DATE DUE			
April 7 '75			

BURT FRANKLIN: RESEARCH & SOURCE WORKS SERIES 867
Philosophy Monograph Series 85

ROUSSEAU

THE REVERIES
OF A SOLITARY

ROUSSEAU.
Engraved by David Martin ; after the painting by Allan Ramsay (1766).
(National Gallery of Scotland, Edinburgh.)

front.

THE
REVERIES
OF A SOLITARY

BY

JEAN JACQUES ROUSSEAU

Translated with an Introduction
by John Gould Fletcher

BURT FRANKLIN
NEW YORK

848.509

R76r

94020

aug 1975

Published by LENOX HILL Pub. & Dist. Co. (Burt Franklin)
235 East 44th St., New York, N.Y. 10017
Originally Published: 1927
Reprinted: 1971
Printed in the U.S.A.

S.B.N. 8337-43589
Library of Congress Card Catalog No.: 73-178094
Burt Franklin: Research and Source Works Series 867
Philosophy Monograph Series 85

Reprinted from the original edition in the Wesleyan Univ.
Library.

CONTENTS

The Reveries of a Solitary

INTRODUCTION

I

CLASSICISM, about which we have heard so much of recent years, is a thing that cannot exist without some settled mythological system. Thus there have been in the world Egyptian classicism, based upon the cult of the dead and its elaboration into Egyptian mythology; Chinese classicism, based upon ancestor-worship and the Confucian cult; Indian classicism, based upon the Vedas and their elaboration into the Upanishads, the epic poems, the system of the Puranas; Greek classicism, based on Homer and Hesiod, and by them transmitted to the lyrists, the dramatists, the sculptors and architects of Athens. Even the ancient Hebrews, though their social and religious order scarcely advanced beyond the tribal stage, and the power of Islam, though it depended for its spread solely on conquest by the sword, had their periods of great classical art. But Christianity, alone, among world-religions has never known a period of independent classic culture, if we except the brief epoch of the twelfth and thirteenth centuries. Up to that

time, Christian culture had largely been a question
of the continuation of the afterglow of pagan culture.
Augustine, Ambrose, Jerome, taught and thought in
terms that Cicero and Virgil had taught them.
Charlemagne expressly had himself crowned Roman
Emperor as a symbol of his control over Europe.   So
great was the power of the unified civilisation Rome
had imposed, that the shadow of the Empire persisted, and the Romanesque basilica repeated the forms
of the Roman senate-house.   It was not until after
the Norman conquest of England, the rise of the
Troubadours and Minnesingers, the Arthurian cycle
of poems, the birth of scholasticism and Gothic
architecture, not until the coming of the Crusades,
that Christian classicism was set going; and it died
in the Renaissance.   The Renaissance began Romanticism, and was itself a wildly Romantic movement.
It resuscitated Plato as against Aristotle, all the old
gods against the Trinity, the fine clothes and jewels
as against secular dirt and squalor.   The only figure
it took over intact from the Middle Ages was the
figure of the Virgin, who—to the scandal of theologians
of the Augustine and Cardinal Newman cast—had
represented in the century of scholasticism the incurable
romanticism that rests undisturbed by the noise of all
classical pedantry.   The Renaissance made more of
the worldliness or unworldliness of Chaucer and
Boccaccio, Ramon Lull and Joachim of Floris, than
it did of all the steely rhythm and filed form of the

2

" Divina Commedia " or the " Dies Iræ." In fact, the Renaissance was perhaps the most Romantic movement that has ever existed. It set men digging the soil of Italy to find forgotten gods; drew Columbus westward to find the Earthly Paradise and Cathay; transformed Wycliff and Luther into rebels, Montaigne, Cervantes, Shakespeare, and Rabelais into heretics and dreamers of Utopia. And from that moment till the opening of the eighteenth century, Christian Europe has never known a classical period. Romanticism found its last champions in Cromwell, Gustavus Adolphus, and that extraordinary creature, Charles XII of Sweden. All three failed, and thanks to the Jesuits, Baroque architecture, Kepler and Newton, the eighteenth century was again a brief period of worldly and sceptical classicism.

But not for long. It is one of the mysteries of history, and marvels of the secret designs of Providence, this question: why Christianity has never achieved a fixed classical standard of taste, values, learning, architecture, and social etiquette, such as was granted in China to the apparently weaker system of Confucianism, in Egypt to the Amon-Ra and Osiris religion, in India to Hinduism, in Japan and Ceylon to Buddhism. Perhaps it was because Jesus believed, far more than any classicist can believe, in liberty. But the last classic period of Christianity, the late seventeenth and early eighteenth centuries, had begun to break down in France from the time Rousseau started to write. The feudal and still more the craft-guilt system of the Middle Ages were unable through rottenness to support society. One of the first acts of the States-General convoked in 1789 was the abolition of the trades-guild system and its privileges, but long before that date the system of the farmers-general, the system of drafted and forced labour (such as had built Versailles) had to be called upon to prevent uprisings and deal with unemployment. Competition between state and state, directed by the rising power of the bourgeois in such countries as England, had already begun. Industrialism, though the steam-engine and machine-technique were not yet invented, was already under way.

From that time onward down to the end of the nineteenth century, and for at least the first ten years of the twentieth, Romanticism has steadily fought on against industrialism and naturalistic science, in alliance with commercial " progress," which even so pronounced an anti-Romanticist as Professor Irving Babbitt says is the greatest enemy of the human race. That Romanticism has done so in the name of individual liberty may be left for consideration in a further section of this Introduction. What must be insisted on here is that the Romantics of the end of the nineteenth century in England, men like Ruskin or William Morris, were not less opposed to machinery and to central machine-made government, than was Rousseau in 1748, when he declared that the savage races were morally and intellectually superior to the civilised.

INTRODUCTION

Unfortunately, however, Romanticism, in order to fight on against the disappearance of the handicraftsman and the landowner and the substitution therefor of the factory-hand and the tenant, backed the wrong horse from the beginning, by espousing the cause of political democracy, now shown to be everywhere a failure. And to investigate the reason why it did so is to study the most impressive error of the whole human mind. Voltaire and Rousseau achieved this error between them—the one by attacking the Church without providing a substitute, thus leading the way to the construction of the Revolutionary Society as a sort of substitute church or crusade within the state (the early Freemasons, the Jacobins, and so on, are all examples of this), the other by declaring that all men had inalienable rights, and that governments thus rested on the consent of the governed—thereby leading the way to the abolition of the hereditary principle in anything, and the creation of the modern megalopolitan democracy.

II

Jean Jacques Rousseau was born on the 28th of June, 1712, three years before " le grand monarque," " le Roi Soleil," Louis XIV, who had done more than any other sovereign of his time to establish a classical order and hierarchy of society, died. Providence, which seems to work often on a principle of vast if unconscious

5

irony, made the most turbulent and disorderly intellectual force of the day the son of a Geneva watchmaker. It was not until Rousseau was nearly forty that he achieved any reputation. Nothing proves better that he was not naturally gifted as a writer than his own account, in the " Confessions," of the enormous difficulties under which he laboured in producing his works. Had it not been for the rupture with Madame de Warens, for which he—by his own reckoning—was largely responsible, he might have lived and died obscure and unfamed. But from the moment when he set foot in Paris in 1741, bearing with him an utterly worthless system of musical notation and some slight skill as a copyist of music, his fate—to which he seems driven despite himself—was settled. Into the tedious, facile, jaded and sated society of his time, the uncouth Genevan, with his love for Plutarch's heroes and his exasperated sensitivity, brought something like a breath from his native mountains. He did not retail *bons mots* ; he had no liking for Jesuitry or intrigue; he was dull to incapacity in a secretaryship which for a brief time he obtained in the Embassy at Venice; and he concealed the fact that his taste was not modelled upon that of society as a whole, by taking as a mistress, not some brilliant member of that society, but an almost illiterate, though well-born girl, Thérèse le Vasseur, whose only claim to his consideration was her unspoilt freshness.

From this time onward, Rousseau's life was a double

warfare—a warfare to justify his character in the eyes of his contemporaries, and a warfare to reform society. It is a curious fact that the works which he wrote to reform society are at the present day dull and tedious, while those which he wrote to justify himself find in every generation their admirers. For every reader of the " Contrat Social," of " Julie," of " Émile," there are probably dozens who intimately know the " Confessions." And another curious fact: it is upon Rousseau's own account of himself that we have to depend in studying him. His enemies, though he counted among them Madame d'Épinay, Grimm, Diderot, and Voltaire, never succeeded in giving such convincing pictures of themselves " stripped bare " as the author of the " Confessions," the " Dialogues," and the work here translated. Their memory depends in great measure upon the ardour and vitality of their great enemy's prose.

Yet it is a striking fact, and one which provides a further proof how little men know about each other, that the world has never been able to make up its mind about Rousseau's character. Was he essentially mean or noble ? Or was he simply crotchety to the point of sheer insanity ? There is but little doubt that from the time " Émile " was condemned by the Parliament of Paris in 1762, and he was driven into exile, Rousseau was afflicted with something closely resembling persecutional mania, and that this mania for finding a plot of his enemies against him on every occasion disfigures the " Confessions " and distorts the present work. But if we are to allow that during the last years of his life he struggled not ignobly with ill-health and misfortune of all sorts, what are we to think of his early years during which he successively deserted Madame de Warens, who had not only constituted herself his protector, but had given him as much as a woman can give to a man, and Madame de Larnage, who, if we are to believe his own account, literally threw herself into his arms ?

The fact is, that Rousseau was a creature of impulse, whose conduct throughout life, and especially with women, displayed a singular mixture of chivalrous desire to protect one weaker than himself, and timidity in venturing to declare himself. Like all the Romantics that have been and will be—for Romanticism is not dead, nor can it die until the last man draws his last breath on this planet—Rousseau may strike the present generation, hardened by the brutal experience of war, of incessant economic struggle and competition, of relaxation of Puritanic standards of conduct into a superficial brilliance of surface and underlying sophistication of impulse, as a mere childlike sentimentalist, less heroic than absurd. I am far from saying that Rousseau would not have been as much out of place in our present state of human society—critical as it is of everything in the past and the present, and yet restlessly seeking some better way of living in the future—as he so obviously was among the more facile and uncomplex ſtandards of the eighteenth century. Yet no one can possibly say that his characſter was not of a piece, consiſtent with itself, and that he himself did not strive to maintain a ſtandard, not only higher than that of his contemporaries, but one to which he himself was not able to conform, according to his own judgment. Of very few, if of any of his contemporaries, could so much be said. Certainly not of Diderot, nor of Voltaire. In contraſt with the worldliness with which they accepted pensions from princes with one hand, while writing libels on society with the other, in contraſt with the facility with which they slipped from one love affair to the other, Rousseau's decision to ſtand aloof from society, as well as his decision to make his union with Thérèse le Vasseur as permanent as possible, has the authentic ring of the heroic. It may be that he was writing in the " Confessions " and later as a man under a grievance, and that, too, a grievance exasperated by ill-health and over-tortured by nerves to the point of obsession. But no one can read his autobiography without realising that under its mingled ſtrains of abasement and passionate self-defence there runs a ſtrain of chivalrous tenderness, of noble regard for life. Less masculine than Cervantes certainly, though equally unfortunate in the society among which he was thrown, Rousseau has, in depiſct-ing himself, given us a figure not unworthy to be set beside Don Quixote. Whether either the legendary Manchegan, or the Jean Jacques of flesh and blood, is a figure that can appear as anything but absurd in this hard workaday world of ours, is a question that the critic need not settle.

What appears most certain is that none of the women with whom Rousseau was brought into contact were in the least worthy of him. Madame de Warens, the friend and protector of his youth, and later his mistress in point of fact, was on the whole the most amiable, tolerant, and well-educated, and his own statement that he was happy in her company is in her favour; but there seems reason to believe that she had previously deserted and robbed her husband, and her looseness in providing herself immediately with a substitute on his departure shows she shared to the full in the laxity of the times. Madame de Larnage was an adventuress, pure and simple. The utmost one can say of Madame d'Épinay is that she offered the impecunious and irritable man of forty-four a shelter at the Hermitage, because she was amused at his gaucheries and half-disposed to love him; and that she withdrew her support because of a *liaison* with Grimm, whose conduct was that of an extreme worldling, tainted with all the scepticism of the eighteenth century. Whether Rousseau was right or wrong in declaring that Grimm had plotted against him, and had drawn Thérèse into the plot, there is no means of knowing exactly; all that one can say is that Madame d'Épinay was an adventurous bluestocking, an equal compound of sensualist and sentimentalist. As for Thérèse le Vasseur, she proved, though Rousseau married her, the most unworthy of them all. There is little doubt that the five children she claimed to have by him and in whose existence she persuaded him to believe, were fictions invented by her mother, to involve him more deeply into the support of her household, which not only contained the mother aforesaid, but a scape-grace son; and though Rousseau himself is at pains to whitewash her conduct, it was both stupid and abominable. Thus we can only say of this unfortunate man whose troubled life ended in poverty and neglect—not without suspicion of suicide —that his prevailing weakness was to be deluded by women. Nor was he any more fortunate with his men friends. With most of them he quarrelled, because they had not either the courage nor the conviction to adopt his principles. Egotistic he was not, nor selfish, nor envious, but he expected too much from the world. And in his latest years he grew into the habit of transferring to others the suspicions he might have more properly felt on account of Thérèse and her appalling family.

We can sum up his character, as well as his misfortunes, by saying that he was a mystic who, instead of following the path of individual self-annihilation in the total consciousness of the world, sought instead the goal of an undifferentiated consciousness in the primal impulse of nature. In doing this, he chose a route which has had more success in the East than in the West, and which is incompatible with a State of achieved and sophisticated intellectual civilisation. For one single St. Theresa, St. John of the Cross, Jacob Behmen, or Jelaluddin Rumi, there have been dozens of failures in Western mysticism: hysterics of the Chateaubriand type, or despairing disillusionists like Baudelaire and the later James Thomson. Rousseau was such a failure, because he could not pass the bounds of pure natural sensation and regard man as an element in the world's order superior to nature, and dependent on a higher plane of inspiration; nor could he reduce the men and women with whom he came into contact back to some more primitive contact with reality. He was thus the very opposite of such mystics as Behmen and Blake, whose aim was to show man and his perceptions as tending towards an infinite order above the bounded and limited domain of natural fact. And because he could find no place in the social order of his day, he became the most severe critic of that order, employing a weapon of such radical sharpness that Voltaire himself declared that he wrote his books against the human race, and Napoleon later uttered the dictum that perhaps it would have been better if neither he nor Rousseau had ever existed.

Yet, despite the fact that he regarded himself as a complete failure, despite the fact that his political, social and economic writings represent a point of view that we can only accept if we are prepared to deny that human history has any significance—for Rousseau's judgments were unhistorical throughout—we find that his influence on European thought has been literally enormous. Not Voltaire, but Rousseau, was the true father of the French Revolution. Jefferson, in the preamble to the American Declaration of Independence, simply repeated the leading thought of the " Contrat Social." A century after the " Discourse on the Arts and Sciences " we find Marx and Engels, in their famous Communist manifesto, varying the thought " Man is born free and is everywhere in chains " into " Workers of the world, unite! You have only your chains to lose, and a world to win." Politically it is not too much to say that the whole of the nineteenth century owes its revolutionary character to the genius of this one man.

And his influence was not less great on literature and the arts. It traversed the young Goethe of the first part of " Faust " and " Werther." It swept through Germany and France a torrent of romanticism. Culminating about 1848, it persisted in various forms down to the outbreak of the war in 1914—though from 1900 onwards its major power was on the wane. Tolstoy, with his theories about art, his gospel of brotherhood, his hatred of civilisation, was one of the last pure Rousseauists to state the gospel in its extreme form—though there are still some pure disciples of Rousseau alive in England, notably Mr. Edward Carpenter. It was only after the war, with Professor Babbitt's " Rousseau and Romanticism," with Jacques

Maritain's "Trois Reformateurs," with Mr. Wyndham Lewis's "The Art of Being Ruled," that criticism of the Rousseau position began.

III

As typical of this criticism, we may take Professor Babbitt with his book on "Rousseau and Romanticism." This book aims at opposing the naturalistic and sentimental ideal of the whole Romantic movement with a classical culture based upon humanistic and positive principles. Apparently the great upholders of this culture are, in Professor Babbitt's view, Matthew Arnold, Aristotle, and Auguste Comte—three men whose somewhat pedantic tediousness and lecture-room manners are accurately reflected in the American teachers' own style. The theories which this true-blue academic, who constantly treats India, China, Egypt and Islam as being inferior to Greece and Rome, puts forward have unfortunately made some stir in the world, as they happened to coincide with the close of the war, when Western culture reached its nadir of disillusionment; therefore we must examine them. Professor Babbitt declares not once but many times in his onslaught against the whole Romantic school, that what the arts must portray is what is normal and centrally representative in human experience, as opposed to what is eccentric and disorganised. But the ideal which Professor Babbitt upholds is as unhistorical at bottom as Rousseau's own defence of savage instinct as opposed to civilised sophistication. What is normal and representative in one age is not what is normal in another. In the thirteenth century it was normal and representative for the man of Western Europe to go on pilgrimage and crusade for the sake of saving his soul; in the twentieth it is normal and representative for him to slay his neighbours with poison gas for the sake of getting more markets, drowning the world with petrol, and thoroughly cheating everybody. That the crusades betrayed underlying imperialistic ambitions, and that the great war was ostensibly advertised as fought for the sake of political democracy, is a matter which does not affect the argument, that what is normal in one age is not normal in another. Without enquiring whether the normal in this age is not debased to such an extent that it has become a menace to all idealism, Professor Babbitt would have the young man of the present day be so modern as to ape Horace, that venal scribbler who played the sedulous ape to Alexandrian culture, or Ovid, the even more facile writer of society verses—poets scarcely on a better level than the late Austin Dobson. To the rest of the world, including Shakespeare and Goethe, both of whom longed for Utopia, he applies his critical scalpel. The fact that Professor Babbitt, in defending normality, upholds, consciously or not, a world of company-promoters, hotel-proprietors, manufacturers of motor-cars, and Zenith Babbitts, seems to have escaped all his contemporaries.

It is, however, not necessary to show that his criticism levelled at Rousseau has no constructive side, in order to prove that Professor Babbitt is mistaken. What is important for us to see is that not one of the great artists of the world, or the great art movements of the world, has sprung from central and normal human experience, or has been dependent on the values of the great bulk of society. The genius, whether he exist in ancient Egypt or China, or to-day in the midst of the industrial community (and to have the former lot was far more preferable than to have to endure the latter), is always exceptional, and works from an experience that is not shared by those about him. This experience is the desire to attain to the absolute, the will to the absolute, in distinction with the great mass of men who are content with the relative. That the "end of ends," in Professor Babbitt's phrase, "is happiness" is expressly denied by all the highest art —by the art of the Gothic cathedrals no less than the art of the Romantic poet. The end of art is religion, whether it be art that unites great bodies of men as in the early period, or art that seeks the path of individual salvation as in the nineteenth century. The moral and the æsthetic are one.[1] That the æsthetic creator is at one period concerned with one side of experience, and at another with another, matters not at all. Human experience itself, far from being sole, unified and constant, as Professor Babbitt would say, is diversified

[1] Wittgenstein: "Tractatus Logico-Philosophicus."

16

to infinity. If it were not so, we should all live to the age of seventy years and be company-promoters or college professors. It is the æsthetic attitude alone that, eternally superior to human experience, draws portions of that experience, from age to age, up into higher harmony, as the light of the sun which illuminates but one portion of the planet at a time, nevertheless illuminates the whole planet. It is through the æsthetic experience alone that we reach out to the beyond and transcend time and space by fusing them. If it be argued that art must ethically submit itself to what is normal and central in human experience, we might as well carry the argument logically one step further and point out that art need never exist at all, since the great majority of people (who are normal and central) are not concerned with it, and do not lift a finger to carry it on. The fact is, that Professor Babbitt has been misled by Goethe, who said that art existed to "make mankind content with their condition." How far "Faust" or "Werther" can make mankind content is not stated. In any case, this argument, used by Goethe to defend the growing Philistinism of his own later years against the "Sturm und Drang" of other artists who were pushing his own youthful attitude further, is false, and all art displays its falsity.

Apart from his upholding of a mummy of classical precept against the striving art of the day, Professor Babbitt's argument against Rousseau becomes very inconclusive. He says that Pascal was right in saying that imagination, which rules the world, is illusory, and right also in saying that reason (which Descartes and his like were forcing on the world in its place) cannot prevail against the Maya-realm of the imagination. Pascal therefore seeks for a harmony with the divine in human intuition. Now, under any unified religion, the intuition of society at large rests on a broad and simple basis. This basis in Christianity was destroyed by the Renaissance, and nothing since has been given to man to supplant it. If the whole of Europe could be induced again to go barefoot to St. James of Compostella or Jerusalem, there might be an awakening of intuition so great as again to result in a new period of cathedral-building and great poetry; but since the religious leaders themselves think in the terms not of revival but of mechanical conversion of everybody to the commercial intuitional basis of unrestricted industrial competition and cheap motors for all, architecture and the arts generally have to suffer. Professor Babbitt himself says that naturalistic science, represented by Darwin and other apostles of the survival of the fittest school, is a greater enemy to man than individualistic Romanticism. But he does not see that what Rousseau and the other Romanticists were fighting against was precisely this naturalistic science in its early stages under Locke, Descartes, and other defenders of the reason against intuition. That Rousseau was obliged, in order to defend intuition, to depend on individual effort as against the tendency

18

of society is a defect not of Romanticism itself, but of the time—and things have grown no better since then. Rather are they much worse, despite Professor Babbitt's concealed attempt to make the mechanical, standardised, uniformised man of the present day " content with his condition."

IV

The position that Rousseau took up was indeed governed by error, but not such an error as Professor Babbitt describes. The error Rousseau made was based on a confusion of the values of society with the values of truth—it is essentially the same mistake as that made by Plato, when he supposed that a human society based on justice and truth could exist. As a matter of fact, we know enough about human societies to know that they are formed and held together not by truth, but by what Thrasymachus, in Plato's "Republic" itself, calls the " instinct of the stronger," and that this instinct is directly dictated by material necessity. Out of necessity comes the faith that a certain course of action is moral for all. The Australian native of the Witchetty Grub tribe performs certain magic rites in order to obtain a supply of his favourite food; the ancient Greek worships Zeus, the fertilising rain that falls into the lap of the earth-mother, in order that Dionysus, the wine-god who comforts man, may be born. Both these actions are motivated by the realisation of necessity symbolising itself as truth. As

19

regards ultimate truth apart from necessity, there is no such thing. And this profound mystical fact, realised by all the great poets, to the point that they spoke not in the positive terms, beloved of all the Babbitts, but rather in parables, paradoxes, and myth-creations, was expressly denied by Rousseau, who unfortunately growing up under the sentimental deism of the day, never grasped Blake's greatest saying: that " there is no natural religion."

If we look at the history of man, we can see that man as soon as he leaves the pure tribal state (which must be regarded as the prehistoric state) adopts one of four forms of government. Each of these forms is modelled on what he conceives the ideal of all possible government to be. Each form claims to come from heaven, and each is an attempt to approximate the government of heaven (which only the exceptional individuals—the medicine-men, priests, and ecstatics—are allowed to know anything about) on earth. The first of these forms of government is that of the only great civilisations that the world has ever known. It is the form that was carried out alike in India, in China, in Egypt, and to a lesser degree by the Hebrews, and by the ancient Incas. Under a government of this sort, men are ruled by a divine king and his descendants and by the priestly caste who are his chief ministers. Under such governments men live divided into castes or colours; there is the priestly caste, which alone has full knowledge of " truth," and which supplies the

State with its great architects, poets, law-makers, musicians, engineers, and magic-makers. Below them is the warrior caste, who defend the State from external attack, the merchants and the work-people. Above them all is the divine king, the " Son of Heaven " or "of the Sun," the representative of the gods on earth, the link of union between the world-order and the order of the universe. Governments of this type have attained the highest possible form of culture that man can achieve; they have also provided happiness for millions of common people over thousands of years. Their great works still remain to confound the petty beings of these latter years. The duration of life of such governments is dependent on the ability of the priesthood to continue the sacrifices unbroken, the maintenance of purity of caste in the royal family (ensured under the Egyptians by the practice of the Pharaohs of marrying their sisters) and the ability of the warriors to ward off invasion from without. They have been the most lasting and beneficent governments man has known.

Less important, because less lasting in effect, have been the great Empires dependent upon military power, and the prowess of the warrior caste. Such governments have been realised by Rome, by the Mogul Empire, the Early Califate, and by the Aztec confederation. Such governments, no longer dependent on the support of a united priesthood, always practise tolerance of religions, but can only survive so long as they are able to push forward the conquest of their neighbours, and so long as they are able to support the severe economic burden of a vast military establishment. They do not achieve such sublime and immense creations of art as do the governments of the first class. Rather do they tend to borrow art from the nations they conquer, and to apply it to their own glorification.

The third class of government comes into existence at the point when religion, as the sense of man's contact with the higher sphere of spiritual values, begins to break down, and human beings lose their desire to achieve great things for the sake of the gods, or to think of their lives as being in any way in contact with higher planes of existence than our earth can show. Under governments of the third class, the programme of representative democracy is applied, not by the small specialised city-state, which, as Rousseau has pointed out, is the only body that has produced under it a vital form of living culture, but by vast industrial communities. England, America, and most of Europe are now controlled in this way. But the government of such communities is always carried on by tradespeople in the interest of the merchant class. Such governments have no programme; they pay as little attention to the dominant sentiments of the people governed as they do to the traditions of the past. They exist in order to bargain, to vulgarise, to compete, to offer the bait of glittering promises to the vast and over-crowded swarms of industrial world-centres. Rome in its later

22

phase—the phase of bread and circuses, of free corn from Egypt and wild-beast shows from all over the world; the phase of nigger dances, exotic cults, and tenement over-crowding—began the list of governments of this specifically "modern" type. England transformed itself from a great military power to an industrial democracy of this sort in the century that lay between 1688 and the French Revolution. America, since 1860, has never known any other kind of government than this shameless thing which calls itself democracy, but which works always in the interest of the plutocracy, and which has neither the honour nor the integrity, nor the religious sense of destiny, to create a culture. This pseudo-democratic, in reality demagogic and plutocratic phase of government, is what Oswald Spengler, the most profound of living historians, calls the "decline of the West"—he might with more appropriateness call it the decline of mankind.

The last class of government possible to man—for with the return to primeval anarchy and disorder no historian need concern himself—is a pure and simple dictatorship of the working-class, resting upon the will of one man drawn out of that class. Such dictatorships are at present being sketched out in Italy, in Russia, in Spain, in Greece, and may very soon come in England, France and Germany. A government of this nature may indeed provide some improvement on a government by a dishonest and bargaining Parliament elected, as all Parliaments must be elected, solely in the interests of the merchant-class, but no means has as yet been devised whereby a dictator can appoint his successors, and such governments offer at the best only intervals of order certain to be broken by intervals of complete anarchy. They are only the desperate last expedients of civilisations exhausted to the point of being unable to struggle against their own disintegration.

Apart from all these is the government represented by the small city-state of antiquity, which can only come into being at a time when all forms of central government have broken down, and can only persist and flourish under special geographical and social conditions. These conditions have only been provided by Nature in four cases: in the case of Ancient Greece, in Japan, in Switzerland, and in the case of the Maya confederation. In all cases, civilisations of high power have existed for a time on the basis of a confederation of such small city-states; but they owed their existence to countries in which means of communication were difficult, sea travel more available than land travel, and where the centres of population lie widely apart.

It was precisely, however, this type of government which Rousseau upheld, misled largely as he was by the retrospective and false romanticism which puts an ideal Greece (largely derived from Plato and Plutarch, and not from the main body of the Greeks themselves) at the very centre of all human striving that has gone on in this planet. Unlike an intelligent modern historian who sees that Egypt, China, India, the

INTRODUCTION

Peruvian-Mayan confederations, the Califate, and to a much lesser degree the Empires of Persia, Rome, and Great Britain, are of the utmost importance in the history of man's ideas and inspirations—unlike this historian, to whom Greece, Japan, and the Mayan confederacy are offshoots, not lacking in charm, but offshoots none the less—Rousseau committed the blunder of supposing that everything had to be modelled on Ancient Athens or Sparta, and was blissfully unaware of the fact that the Ancient Athens and Sparta of reality kept large populations of slaves, and that they owed their independence to geographical conditions impossible to duplicate under the social and economic conditions of the centralised nation-states of his day. Finding the centralised monarchy of his day distasteful in its outlook and methods—and in this he was quite right, for the late French monarchy only ranks as a very poor example of a government of the second order, and does not belong to the early high cultures I have mentioned—Rousseau fell back on the meagre provincialism of the Swiss city-state with its system of direct representative government. And his successors, confusing the devolution of power which he had desperately seized upon, as being the one way out of nationalistic tyranny, the one means of breaking down the absolutism of Louis XIV and his successors, proceeded to apply with their own much more middle-class dreams, his idea to vast tracts of territory by bestowing representative government to

such countries as the United States and the major part
of Europe, thereby bringing about the purely commercial plutocracy which calls itself democracy in all
the Weſtern nations—and which England to her shame
was the firſt to eſtablish.   It is another irony of hiſtory
that through Rousseau, the disillusioned upholder of
the simple Swiss syſtem againſt the complex and
decaying military and nationaliſtic syſtem of the French
—through him the English owe the spread of Imperial-
iſtic and conſtitutional, that is to say plutocratic and
induſtrial government, throughout the world.   What
Rousseau should have been—what he would have been
in our day—is an Eaſterner as againſt a Weſterner, an
upholder of absolutism and caſte againſt mechanical
disruption and disorder.

V

Thus we see that Rousseau, in his harking back to a
condition which can only persiſt under special conditions of soil, climate, and population, effeċtively
killed the decadent French monarchy, and that his
successors were unable to put in its place anything but
the vulgar, time-serving, dishoneſtly bargaining commercial democracy under which the whole of the
Occident is at present fallen, and which rules solely by
means of greed and grab, bread and circuses, glittering
promises to the working-class which are immediately
broken or withdrawn.   The intereſt, therefore, that
we can take in his life and work is entirely the intereſt

26

in the solitary, the man born out of his time, the tragic prophet who saw with clear-sighted pessimism that nothing could save European culture, and still more, religion, upon which all culture rests, except a complete " return to nature."

There are many passages in which Rousseau recalls some of the Hindu or Buddhist hermits of the East, or the early Franciscans. Such, for instance, is his description of the lake of Bienne in the present volume. Like these holy men of old, he lived (but more acutely than they) a life of dissociated consciousness—a waking dream, a contemplative trance—and devoted himself to idleness, pantheism, and observation of the instinct inherent in animal and vegetable states of existence. And it is for this fact that Western democracy, which regards a mountain as a thing to plant a quarry on, a tree as something to turn into wood pulp, a wild animal as something to shoot, stuff, or put in a Zoo, and an ocean as something to defile with petrol—it is for this that we, in the name of a classicism which Aristotle would loathe and Plato shrink back from in horror, condemn him. But Rousseau lived at a time when the type of the holy man, the man who is concerned only with intimations of states which rest beyond mortality, and which only gods perhaps can fully experience, was no longer permitted to exist, except under ecclesiastical or political (and unfortunately both in his day came to the same thing) supervision. There was for him no abiding-place where he might withdraw from the world, be honoured and respected in solitude, and yet remain in intimate counsel and contact with mankind. That state of society does evil, for which countless generations have to pay, which does not provide safety, respect, honour for the holy one who wears simple clothes, prefers the forest to the city, and communes with the gods. Rousseau lived under a government which had already lost wisdom and which was rapidly toppling into that Occidental devil-take-the-hindmost industrial madness which may destroy not only culture and civilisation, but all of mankind in the near future. He, therefore, prepared the vengeance of the gods on the society which had unlearned wisdom; that vengeance was the French Revolution. We who have witnessed the most bloody, unnecessary, cruel and futile war in history, fought in the name of democracy, and won by international plutocratic capital, now struggle under a shadow still greater—a twilight of humanity with scarcely the hope of new dawn. And what we need now is not a single Rousseau, but a whole body of Prophets—a great sacred caste of " superior men " in the sense that Confucius used the word—to bring us forth from the darkness.

1926.

[" The Reveries of a Solitary " is the last of Rousseau's works. Intended as a sequel and complement to the " Confessions," it takes up the story of Rousseau's life at the point where the " Confessions " leaves it—that is to say, with his final exile from Swiss territory in 1765. Rousseau did not live to complete the book which he began in the last year of his life, in 1778.]

(ROUSSEAU'S DEDICATION)

TO

M. DUCLOS,

HISTORIOGRAPHER OF FRANCE,
ONE OF THE FORTY OF THE FRENCH ACADEMY,
AND THE ACADEMY OF BELLES LETTRES.

Suffer, Sir, that your name should appear at the head of this work, which, without you, would not have seen the daylight. This will be my first and unique dedication : may it do you as much honour as I !

I am with all my heart, Sir, your very humble and obedient servant

J. J. ROUSSEAU.

FIRST PROMENADE

HERE am I, then, alone upon the earth, having no brother, or neighbour, or friend, or society but myself. The moſt sociable and loving of human beings has been proscribed by unanimous agreement. They have sought in the refinements of their hatred whatever torment could be moſt cruel to my sensitive soul, and they have violently broken all the links which attached me to them. I would fain have loved men in despite of themselves; they have not been able to conceal themselves from my affeċtion, except by ceasing to be men. They are, then, strangers, unknown, nothing finally for me, because they have wished it. But I, detached from them and from all, what am I in myself? That is what remains to be discovered. Unhappily this search muſt be preceded by a backward glance over my position; that is a mental ſtage through which I muſt necessarily pass in order to arrive at myself.

For fifteen years and more I have been in this ſtrange position, and it ſtill appears to me a dream. I always imagine to myself that an indigeſtion is tormenting me, that I am sleeping badly, and that I am about to awake, eased of my troubles, and to find myself again with my friends. Yes, without doubt, it muſt be that, without perceiving it, I have made a leap from waking to sleep, or from life to death. Drawn, I know not how, from the order of things, I have seen myself precipitated into an incomprehensible chaos, in which I perceive nothing at all; and the more I think of my present state, the less I can understand where I am.

But how could I have foreseen the destiny that awaited me? How can I understand it even to-day when I still suffer from it? Could I, in my good sense, suppose that, one day, I, the same man that I have always been, the same man that I am still, should appear, should be held, as a monster, a poisoner, an assassin; that I should become the horror of the human race, the plaything of the mob; that all the salutation which I should receive from passers-by would be for them to spit in my face; that an entire generation should amuse themselves with burying me alive? When this strange revolution occurred, I was taken by surprise and utterly dumbfounded. My agitation, my indignation, plunged me into a delirium which has taken fully ten years to calm down; and, in that interval, fallen from error to error, from fault to fault, from stupidity to stupidity, I have furnished, by my own imprudences, as many means to the controllers of my destiny, which they have skilfully made use of to render it inalterable.

I have struggled for a long time as violently as vainly. Without skill, without art, without dissimulation, without prudence, frankly, openly, impatiently,

32

carried away by my enthusiasm, I have only succeeded, by struggling, in tying myself up more closely, and in giving my enemies perpetually new holds upon myself which they have taken care not to neglect. Feeling finally that all my efforts were useless, and that I was tormenting myself to pure loss, I have taken up the sole position that remained to me, that of submitting to my destiny, without again revolting against necessity. I have found in this resignation the amends for all my woes, by the tranquillity which it has procured me, and which cannot ally itself with the continual working of a resistance as painful as it was fruitless.

Another thing has contributed to this tranquillity. In all the refinements of their hatred, my persecutors have omitted one which their animosity has made them forget; that of graduating so well the effect of their hatred, that they could have kept up and renewed my sorrows unceasingly, by always inflicting on me some new blow. If they had had the skill to leave open some loophole of hope, they could have held me by this alone. They could have made of me their plaything by some false lure, and made me heart-broken again with new torment caused by deceiving my expectations. But they have exhausted in advance all their own resources; by leaving me nothing, they have taken away everything from themselves as well. The defamation, the derision, the depression, the opprobrium with which they have covered me, are no longer susceptible of increase or of softening; we are both equally incapable—on their side, of aggravating my condition, on my side of dragging myself forth from it. They have been in such haste to bring to its height the measure of my misery, that all of human power, aided by all the ruses of hell, could not add anything to it. Physical pain itself, far from augmenting my trouble, would create a diversion. In wrenching cries from me, perhaps it would spare me groans, and the tortures of my body would suspend those of my heart.

What have I to fear from them still, since all is over ? Not being able to make my state worse, they have not been able to inspire me with any more fears. Inquietude and fright are evils from which they have forever delivered me; that is always a relief. True evils have but little hold upon me; I can always overcome those which I experience, but not those which I fear. My startled imagination combines them, turns them around, extends them, and increases them. Their expectation torments me a hundred times more than their presence, and the menace is more terrible than the blow. As soon as they have arrived, the event, removing from them everything imaginary, reduces them to their own just value. I find them, then, much slighter than I have pictured them; and even in the midst of my suffering, I do not cease to feel relieved. In this state, freed from each new fear and delivered from inquietude, from hope, habit alone suffices to make a situation which nothing can worsen, more supportable from day to day; and to the degree that feeling fades away in time, they have no means to reawaken it. This is the good which my persecutors have done me, by exhausting boundlessly all the traits of their animosity. They have deprived themselves of all power over me, and I can henceforth mock them.

Two months have not gone by since full calm was re-established in my heart. For a long time I had ceased to fear anything, but I still hoped; and this hope, now cherished, now broken, was a snare by which a thousand diverse passions did not cease to agitate me. An event as sad as unforeseen came finally to efface from my heart this feeble ray of hope, and make me see my destiny fixed forever without change here below. From thence, I have resigned myself without reserve and I have rediscovered peace.

As soon as I began to see the plot in all its extent, I lost forever the notion of bringing the public back to my side while I live; and even this return, being no longer reciprocal, would be henceforth quite useless. Mankind may well come back to me, but they will not find me any more. With the disdain they have inspired in me, to mingle with them would be insipid and even a burden; and I am a hundred times more happy in my solitude than I could be in living with them. They have torn from my heart all the sweetnesses of society. These cannot germinate again at my age; it is too late. Let them, therefore, do me good or evil; everything on their part is indifferent to me, and whatever they may do, 'my contemporaries will never be anything to me.

But I still counted upon the future, and I hoped that a later generation examining better both the judgments made by this generation upon me, and its conduct towards me, would easily distinguish the trickery of those who carried it on, and would see me finally as I am. It is this hope which made me write my "Dialogues," and suggested to me a thousand foolish attempts to enable them to pass into posterity. This hope, though distant, kept my soul in the same agitation as when I still searched in this age for a true heart; and my hopes that I did well to rest upon the distant future have equally made me the plaything of men of to-day. I have told in my "Dialogues" the reasons upon which I rested this expectation. I was deceived. I have discovered this, happily, in sufficient time to find still, before my last hour, an interval of full quietness and of absolute repose. This interval began in the epoch of which I am now speaking, and I have reason to believe that it will not be interrupted.

Not many days have gone by since new reflections confirmed to me how much it was a mistake to count upon the return of the public, even in another age; because it is led on, in that which concerns me, by guides who incessantly renew themselves in the bodies of those who have taken a hatred to me. Particular individuals die, but collective bodies do not die. The same passions perpetuate themselves, and their ardent hatred, immortal like the demon that inspires them, has always the same activity. When all my particular friends are dead, the doctors and the Oratorians will live on still; and when I shall not have any persecutors but those two bodies, I may be sure that they will not grant any more peace to my memory after my death than they have granted to my person being alive. Perhaps, by lapse of time, the doctors whom I have really offended, can be pacified: but the Oratorians, whom I have loved, whom I have esteemed, in whom I have had all confidence, and whom I have never offended; the Oratorians, people of the Church and half monks, will be forever implacable; their own iniquity has created my crime, which their self-love will never pardon; and the public, in which they will take care to stir up and reawaken hostility to me incessantly, will not appease itself any more than they.

All is ended for me upon the earth; none can now do me good or evil. There remains for me neither anything to hope for nor to fear in this world, and now I am tranquil at the bottom of the gulf, a poor unfortunate mortal, but as undisturbed as God Himself.

All that is external to me, is now strange henceforward. I have, in this world, neither neighbour, nor kinsmen, nor brothers. I am upon this earth as upon a strange planet, whence I have fallen from that which I inhabited. If I recognise anything about me, it is only some object which is afflicting and torturing to my heart; and I cannot cast my eyes upon that which touches and surrounds me without finding always some subject of disdain which rouses my indignation, or of sorrow which afflicts me. Let me remove, then, from my spirit all the painful objects with which I have occupied myself as sorrowfully as uselessly. Alone for the rest of my life, because I cannot find except in myself consolation, hope and peace, I ought not, and do not wish to occupy myself any longer save with myself. It is in this state that I am taking up the sequel of that sincere and severe examination that I once called my Confessions. I shall consecrate my last days to the study of myself, and to preparing in advance the account which I shall not be slow to give of myself. Let me devote myself entirely to the sweetness of speaking with my own soul, because that is the only thing of which men cannot rob me. If, by force of reflecting upon my inward propensities, I succeed in putting these in order and correcting the evil that may remain there, my meditations will not be entirely useless, and although I shall not be good for anything upon this earth, I shall not have lost entirely my last days. The leisures of my daily walks have often been filled with delightful contemplations of which I regret having lost the memory. I shall set down in writing those which may still come to me; each time that I reread them will give me new pleasure. I shall forget my sufferings, my persecutors, my opprobrium, in dreaming of the reward which my heart has merited.

FIRST PROMENADE

These leaves will not be, properly speaking, anything but a formless journal of my reveries. There will be much concerning myself, because a solitary who reflects occupies himself necessarily much with himself. For the rest, all the strange ideas which pass through my head in walking about will equally find a place. I shall say that which I have thought exactly as it has come to me, and also with as little linking together as the ideas of yesterday ordinarily have with those of the day following. But there will always result a new understanding of my nature and my humour, through the knowledge of the sentiments and the thoughts on which my spirit feeds daily, in this strange state in which I am. These leaves can then be regarded as an appendix to my " Confessions," but I do not give them this title, as I have nothing more to say which can merit being said. My heart has been purified in the crucible of adversity, and I scarcely find, in sounding it carefully, anything that remains of a reprehensible tendency. What could I have still to confess, when all my earthly affections are torn away ? I have nothing to praise or blame myself for; I am nothing henceforward among men, and that is all that I can be, having no more a real relation or a veritable companionship with them. Not being able to do any good that does not turn into evil, not being able to act without injury to another or to myself, to abstain has become my unique duty, and I shall fulfil it as much as is in me. But, in this idleness of body, my soul is still active; it still produces sentiments and thoughts, and its inner and moral life seems to be increased by the death of every earthly and temporal interest. My body is nothing to me but an embarrassment, but an obstacle, and I shall in advance disengage myself from it as much as I can.

A situation so singular as this deserves assuredly to be examined and described, and it is to this examination that I have devoted my last leisure. To do it with success, it is necessary to proceed with order and method; but I am incapable of this labour, and it would even remove me from my goal, which is to render an account to myself of the modifications of my soul and of their successions. I shall carry out upon myself to a certain extent the operations which the physicists make upon the air, to understand its daily state. I shall apply the barometer to my soul, and these operations well directed and for long repeated will furnish me with results as sure as those of science. But I shall not extend my enterprise so far. I shall content myself with keeping a register of my operations, without seeking to reduce them into system. I shall carry out the same enterprise as Montaigne, but with a goal entirely contrary to his, because he did not write his Essays except for others, and I do not write my reveries except for myself. If, in my extreme age, at the approach of death, I remain, as I hope, in the same mood as I am now, the reading of my reveries will recall to me the pleasure that I tasted in writing them, and thus making reborn for me times gone by, will, so to say,

redouble my existence. In spite of men I shall still
enjoy the charm of society, and I shall live decrepit with
myself in another age, as if I were living with a younger
friend.

I wrote my "Confessions" and my "Dialogues" in a
continual anxiety about the means of snatching them
from the rapacious hands of my persecutors, in order to
transmit them, if it were possible, to other generations.
The same disquiet does not torment me any more as
regards this work; I know it will be useless; and the
desire of being better known among men having been
extinguished in my heart leaves nothing but a profound
indifference to the lot both of my true writings and
of the testimonies to my innocence, which already
perhaps have been all destroyed for ever. Let them
spy upon what I am doing, let them worry themselves
about these leaves, let them seize upon them, suppress
them, falsify them, everything is the same to me henceforward. I do not hide or display them. If they are
taken away from me in my lifetime, I cannot be robbed
of the pleasure of having written them, nor of the
memory of their contents, nor of the solitary meditations of which they are the fruit and of which the source
cannot be extinguished except with my soul. If,
upon my first calamities, I had not turned against
my destiny, and had taken up the position which I
take to-day, all the efforts of men, all their frightful
intrigues, would have been without effect upon me, and
they would not have troubled my repose by all their

plots, any more than they can trouble it henceforward by all their successes. Let them rejoice to their hearts' content at my disgrace, they will not prevent me from rejoicing in my innocence, and from ending my days in peace despite them all.

SECOND PROMENADE

HAVING, then, formed the project of describing the habitual state of my soul in the most strange position in which a mortal can ever find himself, I saw no way more simple and more sure of executing this enterprise than to make a faithful record of my solitary walks and of the reveries that fill them, when I leave my head entirely free and let my ideas follow their bent without resistance and without trouble. These hours of solitude and meditation are the only ones of the day in which I am fully myself and for myself, without diversion, without obstacle, and where I can truly say I am that which nature has designed.

I soon felt that I had delayed too long in executing this project. My imagination, already less alive, does not enkindle as before at the contemplation of the object which animates it; I am less drunken with the delirium of reverie; there is more of reminiscence than of creation in that which it now produces; the spirit of life is extinguished in me by degrees, my soul does not leap out any more except with a struggle from its narrow envelope, and, lacking the hope of the state to which I aspire because I feel I have right to it, I do not exist now except in memories; so in order to

43

contemplate myself before my decline, it is necessary that I should go back at least some years to the time when, losing all hope here below and not finding more food for my heart upon earth, I accustomed myself little by little to nourish it with its own substance and to seek all its pasturage within myself.

This resource, of which I learned too late, became so fecund that it soon sufficed to compensate me for everything. The habit of entering into myself made me lose finally the feeling and even the remembrance of my evils. I learned thus by my own experience that the source of true happiness is in ourselves, and that it did not depend upon men to make miserable him who knows how to will to be happy. For four or five years, I tasted habitually these internal delights which loving and tender souls find in contemplation. These ravishments, these ecstasies, that I found sometimes in walking thus alone, were enjoyments which I owed to my persecutors: without them, I could not have ever found nor known the treasures which I carried within myself. In the midst of so much richness, how keep a faithful register? In trying to recall to myself so many sweet reveries, instead of describing them I fell back into them again. It is a state which the memory brings back and which one would soon cease to understand by ceasing entirely to feel.

I experienced this effect in the Promenades which followed the project of writing the sequel to my "Con-

fessions," above all in one which I am about to speak
of, and in which an unforeseen accident came to break
the thread of my ideas and to give them for some
time another direction.

On Thursday, October 24, 1776, after dinner I
followed the boulevards up to the Rue du Chemin-Vert,
by which I gained the heights of Ménilmontant; and
from there, taking the paths across the vineyards and
meadows, I followed as far as Charonne the smiling
landscape which unites the two villages: then I made
a détour to return to the same meadows, by taking
another road. I amused myself by going over them
with that pleasure and interest which agreeable sites
have always given me, stopping sometimes to identify
plants in the grass. I perceived two which I see very
rarely around Paris, and which I found very abundant
in this district. One is the *Picris hieracoides* of the
composite group, and the other the *Bupleurum falcatum*
of the umbelliferous family. This discovery delighted
and amused me for a long time, and finished by
that of a plant still more rare, especially in a high
country, that is to say, the *Cerastium aquaticum*, which,
despite the accident which befell me the same day,
I found again in a book which I had in my pocket,
and put into my herbarium.

Finally, after having gone over in detail many
other plants which I saw still in flower, and whose
aspect and classification which were familiar to me
nevertheless still gave me pleasure, I quitted little

by little these slight observations in order to yield myself
to the impression, not less agreeable, but more touching, which the whole of the landscape made upon me.
For some days the vintage had been harvested; the
walkers from the city had already gone home, the
peasants also were quitting the fields for the labour of
the winter. The country, still green and smiling,
but unleafed in part, and already almost desert, offered
everywhere the image of solitude and of the approach
of winter. There resulted from its aspect a mixed
impression, sweet and sad, too analogous to my age and
lot that I should fail to make the application to myself. I
saw myself at the decline of an innocent and unfortunate
life; the soul still full of lively sentiments, and the
spirit still ornamented with some flowers, but already
withered by sadness and dried up in *ennui*. Alone
and abandoned, I felt the chill of the first frosts,
and my failing imagination did not people my solitude
any more with beings formed according to my own
heart. I said to myself with a sigh: What have I
done here on earth? I was made for living, and I
am dying, without having lived. At least this has not
been my fault, and I shall carry back to the Author
of my being, if not the offering of good works which
men have not allowed to me, at least a host of good but
frustrated intentions, of sentiments healthy but made of
no effect, and of a patience above the contempt of men.
I grew tender at these reflections; I went over again the
movements of my soul since youth, and during my

mature age, since I have been sequestered from the society of men, and during the long retreat in which I must finish my days. I went back with pleasure over all the affections of my heart, over all its attachments, so tender, but so blind, over the ideas less sad than consoling, with which my spirit has been nourished for some years, and I prepared to recall these sufficiently to describe them with a pleasure almost equal to that which I had taken in yielding myself to them. My afternoon passed in these peaceful meditations, and I was returning very content with my day, when, in the midst of my reverie, I was drawn out of it by the event which it remains for me to describe.

I was, about six o'clock, on the descent from Ménilmontant, almost face to face with the Galant Jardinier, when certain persons who were walking in front of me having been suddenly swept aside, I saw rushing towards me a great Danish dog, which flying at full speed in front of a carriage, had no time to check its speed or to turn aside when it perceived me. I judged that the sole means that I had to avoid being thrown down to earth was to make a great leap, so that the dog should pass under me while I was in the air. This idea, more swift than the lightning, and which I had not even the time to reason out or to execute, was the last before my accident. I did not feel the blow, nor the fall, nor anything of what followed, up to the moment when I came to myself.

REVERIES OF A SOLITARY

It was almoſt night when I came back to consciousness. I found myself between the arms of three or
four young people who told me what had happened.
The Danish dog, not having been able to check its
onrush, was precipitated upon my two legs, and ſtriking
me with its body and its speed, made me fall head
foremoſt; the upper jaw, bearing the whole weight of
my body, ſtruck upon a very hard pavement, and the
fall was the more violent because, the road being down-
hill, my head was thrown down lower than my feet.
The carriage to which the dog belonged followed
immediately, and would have passed over my body if
the coachman had not reined in his horses upon the
inſtant.

ᵗThat is what I learned from the recital of those
who had picked me up and who held me ſtill when I
came to myself. The ſtate in which I found myself
in that inſtant was too singular not to make a description of it here.

The night was coming on. I perceived the sky,
some ſtars, and a little grass. This firſt sensation was
a delicious moment. I did not feel anything except
through them. I was born in that inſtant to life, and
it seemed to me that I filled with my light exiſtence all
the objeꞓs which I perceived. Entirely given up to
the present moment, I did not remember anything;
I had no diſtinꞓ notion of my individuality, not the
leaſt idea of what had happened to me; I did not
know who I was nor where I was; I felt neither evil

nor fear, nor trouble. I saw my blood flowing as I might have looked at a brooklet, without dreaming even that this blood in any way belonged to me. I felt in the whole of my being a ravishing charm, to which, each time that I think of it, I find nothing comparable in the whole action of known pleasures.

They asked me where I lived: it was impossible for me to say. I asked where I was; they said on the High Cliff; it was as if they said to me: on Mount Atlas. It was necessary for me to ask successively the country, the city, and the quarter where I was: still this did not suffice for me to recollect myself; it was necessary for me to walk the whole distance from there to the highroad in order to recall my home and my name. A gentleman whom I do not know, and who had the charity to accompany me for a time, learning that I lived so far away, advised me to take a cab at the Temple to carry me back home. I walked quite well, very softly, without feeling either pain or wound, although I kept spitting blood. But I had an icy shiver which made my loose teeth rattle in a very un-comfortable way. Arrived at the Temple, I thought that, because I walked without trouble, it was better worth while to continue my route, on foot, than to expose myself to perishing of cold in a cab. I thus covered the half-a-league which lay between the Temple to the Rue Platière, walking without trouble, avoiding the obstructions, the carriages, choosing and following my road as well as I could have done in full health. I arrived; I opened the lock which had been put upon the street-door, I went up the stairway in darkness, and I finally entered my house without other accident than my fall and its sequels, of which I did not feel anything even then.

The cries of my wife upon seeing me made me understand that I had been more injured than I supposed. I passed the night without understanding or feeling my accident. This is what I felt and found in the morning. I had the upper lip split inside up to the nose; on the outside the skin had preserved it better, and prevented the total separation; four teeth were bent back in the upper jaw, the whole of that part of the face which covered it extremely swollen and bruised, the right thumb sprained and very swollen, the left thumb severely cut, the right arm sprained, the left knee also very swollen, while a strong and painful contusion forbade me totally to bend it. But, with all this fracas, nothing broken, not even a tooth; a good fortune which seemed almost a miracle in a fall like that.

This is faithfully the story of my accident. In a few days this story was spread about Paris, so changed and disfigured, that it was impossible to recognise anything of it. I should have counted in advance upon this metamorphosis; but there were joined to it so many bizarre circumstances, so many obscure remarks and reticences accompanied it; people spoke to me about it with an air so smilingly discreet, that all these mysteries disquieted me. I have always hated dark secrets; they inspire me naturally with a horror which those with which men have surrounded me for so many years have not been able to diminish. Amid all the singularities of this epoch I took notice of but one, which is sufficient to form an estimate of the others.

M——, with whom I have never had any relation, sent his secretary to enquire the news of me, and to make me pressing offers of services which did not appear to me, under the circumstances, of much use for my recovery. His secretary did not cease to press me very strongly to make use of his offers, going so far as to say that if I did not trust him, I could write directly to M——. This great eagerness and the air of confidence which was joined to it, made me understand that there was underneath it some mystery which I sought vainly to penetrate. It did not take much to frighten me; above all, in the state of agitation which my accident, and the fever added to it, had put my head. I yielded myself up to a thousand uneasy and sad conjectures, and all that happened about me caused me to make remarks which revealed rather the delirium of fever than the cool head of a man who does not take any interest in anything.

Another event came to complete the disturbance of my tranquillity. Madame X. had sought me for some years, without my being able to divine why. A great number of small presents, and frequent visits, without object and without pleasure, showed me a secret aim in all this, but did not tell me what it was. She spoke of a romance which she wished to write, in order to present it to the Queen. I said what I thought of women authors. She gave me to understand that this project had as its object the re-establishment of her fortune, for which she needed protection: I had nothing to reply to that. She said afterwards that, not having been able to obtain access to the Queen, she had determined to give her book to the public. There was no reason to give her advice which she did not ask of me, and which she would not have followed. She spoke of showing me the manuscript beforehand. I begged her to do nothing of the sort, and she did nothing.

One fine day, during my convalescence, I received from her this book printed, and even bound, and I saw in its preface such gross praises of me, so badly displayed and done with such affectation, that I was disagreeably surprised. Coarse flattery which makes itself felt, never is allied with benevolence: my heart could never be deceived on that score.

Some days afterwards, Madame X. came to see me with her daughter. She told me that her book was making a great stir on account of a note which had attracted attention to it; I had scarcely observed this note on rapidly going over the romance. I reread it after the departure of Madame X.; I examined the turn of phrase; I believed that I had found the motive of her visits, of her flatteries, of the gross overpraise of her preface; and I judged that all this had no other reason than to dispose the public to attribute to me the note, and in consequence attract the censure that it might draw down upon its author under the circumstances in which it was published.

I had no means of destroying this rumour and the impression it might make; and all that I could do was not to support it by suffering the continuation of the vain and showy visits of Madame X. and of her daughter. To obtain this result, here is the note I wrote the mother:

" Rousseau, not receiving any author in his house, thanks Madame X. for her kindness, and prays her not to honour him any more with her visits."

She replied to me with a letter honest enough in form, but phrased like all those which people write to me under similar circumstances. I had barbarously thrust a dagger into her feeling heart, and I should realise, by the tone of her letter, that having sentiments so lively and so true for me, she would not endure this rupture without dying. It is true that directness and frankness in everything are frightful crimes in this world; and I appear to my contemporaries malicious and fierce, when I have shown no other crime in their eyes than not to be so false and perfidious as they.

I had already gone out many times, and I even walked frequently in the Tuileries, when I saw, from the astonishment of many of those who encountered me, that there was still, in regard to me, some other news that I did not know. I learned finally that the public rumour was that I was dead of my fall; and this rumour spread so rapidly and so obstinately, that more than fifteen days after I learned it, it was spoken of at the Court as a certain fact. The Courier of Avignon, as someone took pains to write me, did not fail to anticipate on this occasion the tribute of outrages and indignities which were being prepared for my memory after death, in the form of a funeral oration.

This news was accompanied with a circumstance still more singular which I only learned by chance, and of which I have not been able to know any detail. It is that a subscription had been opened at the same time to print the manuscripts which might be found in my house. I understood by this that a collection of fabricated writings were being kept ready expressly for the purpose of attributing them to me after my death; because to think that anyone would print faithfully any of those which would be actually found, was a stupidity which would not enter into the mind of a sensible man, and against which fifteen years of experience have only too much warned me.

These observations, made stroke on stroke, and followed by many others which were scarcely less astounding, nevertheless startled my imagination which I thought deadened; and these dark scandals, which were being reinforced without relaxation about me, reawakened all the horror they naturally inspired in me. I wearied myself in making a thousand explanations of all this, and in seeking to understand the mysteries which had been made inexplicable for me. The one invariable result of all these riddles was the confirmation of my previous conclusions, that is, I knew that the destiny of my person and of my reputation having been fixed by agreement by all the present generation, no effort on my part could enable me to escape them, because it was impossible for me to transmit any record to other ages without letting it pass through this age by means of hands interested in suppressing it.

But this time I went further. The amassing of so many fortuitous circumstances, the elevation of all my most cruel enemies, led on, so to say, by fortune, all those who governed the State, all those who directed public opinion, all the people in office, all the men in credit chosen from among the best of those who have some secret animosity against me, to act together in the common plot; this universal agreement was too extraordinary to be purely fortuitous.

A single man who would have refused to be an accomplice, a single event that might have been contrary to it, a single unforeseen circumstance that would have made an obstacle to the scheme, would have sufficed to make it fail. But all the wills, all the fatalities, fortune, and all the revolutions have strengthened the work of men; and an agreement so striking, which appears a prodigy, could not let me doubt but that its full success was written in the eternal decrees. Multitudes of special observations, whether in the past or the present, have confirmed me so far in this opinion, that I cannot prevent myself from regarding henceforth as one of the secrets of heaven, impenetrable to human reason, the same work which I did not envisage up to now except as the fruit of the maliciousness of men.

This idea, far from being cruel and heart-breaking to me, consoles me, tranquillises me, and aids me in resigning myself. I do not go so far as St. Augustine, who was consoled for being damned, if that were the will of God: my resignation comes from a source less disinterested, it is true, but not less pure, and more worthy, in my opinion, of the perfect Being that I adore.

God is just, He wills that I should suffer, and He knows that I am innocent. There is the motive of my confidence; my heart and my reason cry out that it will never deceive me. Let men and destiny do what they can; let us learn to suffer without complaint; all must in the end return to order, and my turn will come sooner or later.

THIRD PROMENADE

I GROW old while forever learning.

Solon often repeated this verse in his old age. There is a sense in which I can also say it in mine; but it is a very sad knowledge, this, which experience has made me acquire for twenty years: ignorance is still preferable. Adversity without a doubt is a great master; but this master makes his lessons cost dearly, and often the profit one obtains from them is not worth the price one has paid. For the rest, before one has obtained all this acquisition by means of such tardy lessons, the correct time for using them has passed away. Youth is the time to study wisdom; old age is the time to practise it. Experience always instructs, I admit: but it does not profit except for the space of time that one has before one.

Is it the time, at the moment when one has to die, to learn how one should have lived ?

What avails knowledge so late and painfully acquired on my destiny, and on the passions of others, of which my destiny is the result ? I have not learned to understand men better except through feeling more keenly the misery into which they have plunged me; nor has this knowledge, though discovering all their snares, enabled me to avoid them. Why did I not remain always in the stupid but pleasing confidence which made me for so many years the prey and the plaything of my ostensible friends, while enveloped in all their plots I was without the least suspicion? I was their dupe and their victim, it is true; but I believed myself to be loved by them, and my heart rejoiced in the friendship which they had inspired in me, while attributing to them as much for myself. These sweet illusions are destroyed. The sad truth, that time and reason have unveiled to me, in making me feel my misfortune, has made me see that it is without remedy, and that there remains nothing for me but to resign myself. Thus all the experiences of my age are for me, in my state, without present utility and without profit for the future.

We enter into the struggle at our birth, we go out of it upon our death. What does it serve to grasp how we can better manage our lives, when we are at the end of our career? There is nothing to think about, then, but how we will pass out of life. The study of an old man, if there is anything still for him to do, is solely to learn to die; and it is precisely this which one does least at my age: one thinks of everything except that. All old men hold more firmly to life than children, and go out of it with worse grace than young people. It is because, all their work having been for this life, they see at the end that they have lost their trouble. All their needs, all their goods, all the fruits of their laborious struggles, they abandon when they pass away. They have not dreamed of acquiring anything during their lives which they can carry away at their death.

I said all this when it was time to say it; and if I have not better known how to obtain an advantage from my reflections, it was not for lack of making them in time, and of having well digested them. Thrown since my childhood into the whirlpool of the world, I learned in good time, by experience, that I was not made to live there, and that I should never attain to the state of which my heart felt the need. Ceasing then to seek among men the happiness which I felt I was unable to find there, my ardent imagination leapt already beyond the span of my life, hardly begun, as from a plot of ground that was strange to me, to rest itself upon a tranquil position where I could settle myself.

This sentiment, fostered by education from my infancy, and reinforced throughout my life, by the long web of miseries and misfortunes that have filled it, has made me seek, at all times, to understand the nature and destiny of my being with more interest and care than I have found in any other man. I have seen many who philosophised more learnedly than I, but their philosophy was, so to speak, foreign to them. Wishing to be more learned than others, they studied the universe to know how it was arranged, as they might have studied some strange machine which they had remarked, out of pure curiosity. They studied human nature to be able to speak of it wisely, but not to know themselves; they worked to instruct others, but not to enlighten themselves from within. Many of them did not wish anything but to write a book, it mattered not what, provided it was well received. When their own book was done and published, the contents did not interest them in any way, except to have what it said adopted by others, and to defend it in case it was attacked; but for the rest, without drawing anything for their own proper use therefrom, without worrying whether this content was false or true, provided it was not refuted. For myself, when I desired to learn anything, it was to know myself and not to teach; I have always believed that before instructing others, it was necessary to begin by knowing enough for oneself; and of all the studies that I have attempted to make in my life in the midst of men, there is scarcely one that I might not have made equally alone on a desert island where I might have been confined for the rest of my days. That which we should do depends much on that which we should believe; and in all that does not depend upon the first needs of nature, our opinions are the guide of our actions. On this principle, which was always mine, I have sought often and long to understand the true end of life in order to direct the occupation of my own, and I was soon consoled for my small aptitude for guiding myself skilfully through the world, by feeling that it is not necessary to seek this aim.

Born in a family devoted to morals and piety, brought up afterwards with gentleness at the house of a minister who was full of wisdom and religion, I received from my earliest infancy principles, maxims —others would say prejudices—which have never entirely abandoned me. While still a child, and left to myself, flattered by caresses, seduced by vanity, deceived by hope, forced by necessity, I became Catholic, but I always remained Christian; and soon, won over by habit, my heart attached itself sincerely to my new religion. The teachings and example of Madame de Warens confirmed me in this attachment. The solitude of the fields where I passed the flower of my youth, the study of good books to which I gave myself up entirely, reinforced near her my natural dispositions and affectionate sentiments and made me devout almost in the manner of Fénelon. Meditation in retreat, study of nature, the contemplation of the universe, force a solitary to direct himself incessantly towards the author of things and to seek with a tender restlessness the end of all that he sees and the cause of all that he feels. When my destiny cast me into the torrent of the world, I did not find anything there which could flatter my heart for a moment. Regret for my sweet leisure followed me everywhere and cast indifference and disgust upon all that which could be found within reach of my ambition, able to carry me to fortune and honour. Uncertain in my restless desires, I hoped little, I obtained less, and I felt, in the flashes even of prosperity that when I had obtained all that I believed I sought, I had not yet found there the

happiness for which my heart was eager without knowing how to discern its object. Thus all contributed
to detach my affections from this world, even before
the misfortunes that were to make me entirely strange
to it. I attained the age of forty years, floating between
poverty and fortune, between wisdom and heedlessness,
full of vices of habit without any evil tendency in my
heart, living at hazard without principles decided upon
by my reason, and distracted from my duties without
despising them, but often without really understanding
them.

From my youth up I fixed this epoch of forty years
as the term of my efforts at success, and as that of my
ambitions in all respects; fully resolved, when that
age was attained, and in whatever situation I found
myself, not any more to struggle on to emerge from
it, but to pass the rest of my days in living from day
to day, without occupying myself any more with the
future. The moment having come, I executed this
project without trouble, and though then my fortune
seemed to be reaching a more secure position, I renounced it, not only without regret, but with real
pleasure. In delivering myself from all these snares,
from all these vain hopes, I yielded myself fully to heedlessness and to the repose of spirit which was always
my most dominant taste and my most lasting aim.
I quitted the world and its pomps. I renounced all
fine apparel; no more sword, no more watch, no more
white stockings, gold thread, coiffure; a simple periwig,

a good coarse suit of cloth; and better than all this, I uprooted from my heart the cupidities and the covetings which gave a value to all that I had quitted. I renounced the post which I then occupied, for which I was in no way fitted, and I set myself to copying music at so much the page, an occupation for which I had always a decided taste.

I did not limit my reform to external things. I felt that this reform itself exacted another more painful doubtless, but more necessary, in my opinion; and, resolved not to make it twice, I undertook to submit my inner being to a severe examination which would regulate it for the rest of my life, making it such as I wished to find it upon my death.

A great revolution which came about in me, another moral world which unveiled itself to my gaze; the senseless judgments of men, of which, without foreseeing how I would be the victim, I began to feel the absurdity; the ever-increasing need of another good than literary glory, of which scarcely the breath had struck me when I was already disgusted; the desire finally to follow for the rest of my career a road less uncertain than that in which I had already passed the better half of my life; everything obliged me to undertake this great review of myself of which I had long felt the need. I undertook it then, and I neglected nothing that was in my power in order to execute this enterprise well.

It is from this epoch that I can date my entire

renunciation of the world, and this vivid taste for solitude, which has not quitted me from that time onward. The work which I undertook could not be executed except in an absolute retreat; it demanded long and peaceful meditations which the tumult of society would not allow. This forced me to take up for a time another way of living in which I found myself so happy that, not having interrupted it since then except by force and for a few moments, I resumed it with all my heart, and limited myself to it without difficulty, as soon as I could; so when finally men reduced me to living alone, I found that in banishing me to make me miserable, they did more for my happiness than I knew how to do myself.

I yielded myself to the labour that I undertook with a zeal proportioned both to the importance of the thing and to the need which I felt I had for it. I lived then with the modern philosophers who scarcely resemble the ancients: in place of easing my doubts and fixing my irresolutions, they had shaken all the certitudes that I thought I had upon the points which it most imported me to know: because, ardent missionaries of Atheism and very imperious dogmatists, they did not endure without anger, that on any point that might exist anyone dared to think otherwise than they. I defended myself often very weakly through dislike for dispute, and through small talent to sustain it; but never did I adopt their desolating doctrine: and this resistance to men so intolerant, who moreover had their own aims, was not one of the least causes for attracting their animosity.

They did not persuade, but they disquieted me. Their arguments shook me, without ever convincing; I did not find a good answer, but I felt there should be one. I accused myself less of error than of feebleness, and my heart replied to them better than my reason.

I said finally: Shall I allow myself to be eternally swayed by the sophisms of the best-reputed talkers, of whom I am not even sure that the opinions they preach, and which they have so much ado to get adopted by others, are even theirs for themselves? Their passions which govern their doctrine, their interest to have this or that believed, makes it impossible to know what they believe themselves. Can one seek for good faith in the leaders of a party? Their philosophy is for others; it is necessary to have one for myself. Let me seek then with all my strength while it is still time, in order to have a fixed rule of conduct for the rest of my days. Here I am in the maturity of my age, in all the force of my understanding; already I approach my decline; if I wait still, I shall no longer have, in my tardy delibera- tion, the use of all my forces; my intellectual faculties will have already lost their activity; I shall do less well that which I can do to-day in the best possible manner; let me grasp this favourable moment: it is the period of my external and material reform, let it be also that of my intellectual and moral reform. Let me fix once and for all my opinions, my principles: and let me be for the rest of my life that which I find I ought to be after having well thought upon it.

I carried out this project slowly and after several attempts, but with all the effort and all the attention of which I was capable. I felt strongly that the repose of the rest of my days and my whole fate depended upon it. I found myself at first in such a labyrinth of embarrassments, of difficulties, of objections, of tortuosities, of darkness, that twenty times tempted to abandon all, I was ready, renouncing vain searches, to hold, in my deliberations, to the rules of common prudence, without searching further into principles which I had so much trouble to unravel: but this prudence itself was so foreign to me, I felt myself so little apt to acquire it, that to take it for my guide was nothing less than to attempt without rudder or compass in the midst of seas and storms, to reach an almost inaccessible lighthouse which did not indicate to me any harbour.

I persisted: for the first time in my life I had courage, and I owe to its strength the ability I had to sustain the horrible destiny which from thenceforth began to envelop me, although I had not the least suspicion of it. After the most ardent and most sincere researches that perhaps had ever been made by any mortal, I decided for the rest of my life upon the feelings which it was necessary for me to have; and if I may have been deceived in my results, I am sure at least that my mistake

cannot be imputed to me as a crime: for I have made
every effort to protect myself from it. I do not doubt,
it is true, that the prejudices of my childhood and the
secret wishes of my heart have made the balance incline
to the side most consoling to myself. It is with difficulty that one forbids oneself from believing what one
seeks with so much ardour, and who can doubt that
the interest of admitting or rejecting the judgments
of another life determines the faith of most men according to their hope or their fear ? All this might fasci-
nate my judgment, I admit, but could not alter my good
faith; for I feared to deceive myself in everything. If
all consisted in the usages of this life, it would be important to know them in order to choose at least the
best lot that was in my power while it was still
time, and not to be entirely duped. But that which
I had the most to fear from the world, in my then state
of mind, was to risk the eternal fate of my soul for
the enjoyment of the goods of this world, which have
never appeared to me of great value.

I admit that I did not always answer to my satisfaction all the difficulties which have embarrassed
me, and with which our philosophers had so often
disturbed my ears. But, resolved to decide finally
upon matters of which the human intelligence has so
little grasp, and finding on all sides impenetrable
mysteries and insoluble objections, I adopted directly
in each question the sentiment which appeared to me
the best established, without stopping at objections

which I could not resolve, but which were contra-
dicted by other objections not less strong in the opposite
system. The dogmatic tone in these matters does not
suit any except charlatans; but it is necessary to have a
sentiment for oneself and to choose it with all the
maturity of judgment that one can bestow. If despite
this we fall into error, we shall not in justice bear the
suffering, because we have not the guilt. This is
the unshakable principle which is at the base of my
security.

The result of my painful researches was practically
that which I gave out in the profession of faith of the
Savoyard Vicar,[1] a work unworthily prostituted and
profaned in the present generation, but which some
day may make a revolution among men, if ever good
sense and good faith are born again among them.

From that time on, resting tranquilly in the principles which I have adopted after a meditation so long
and so thought out, I have made it an unchangeable
rule of my conduct and my faith, without any more
disquieting myself either upon the objections which
I have been unable to resolve, or on those which I
have been unable to foresee, and which present themselves newly from time to time to my spirit. They have
disquieted me sometimes, but they have never shaken
me. I have always said: All this is nothing but

[1] The profession of faith of the Savoyard Vicar appears in the
novel of "Émile," which was condemned by the Parlement de Paris
in 1762.

quibbles and metaphysical subtleties, which are of no weight after the fundamental principles adopted by my reason, confirmed by my heart, and which all carry the seal of interior assent in the silence of my passions. In matters so superior to human understanding, can an objection which I cannot resolve reverse the whole body of solid doctrine, so well linked and formed with so much meditation and care, so well appropriated to my reason, to my heart, to all my being, and reinforced with the inner assent which I feel to be lacking to all others ? No; vain arguments do not destroy ever the agreement which I perceive between my immortal being and the constitution of this world, and the physical order that I see reigning there; I have found in the corresponding moral order, the system of which is the result of my searches, those footholds which I need to support the miseries of my life. In every other system, I should live without resources and die without hope; I should be the most miserable of creatures. Let me hold fast to that which alone suffices to render me happy, in despite of fortune and of men.

This deliberation and the conclusion I drew from it, do they not seem to have been dictated by Heaven itself to prepare me for the destiny which awaited me, and to put me into the condition of enduring it ? What might I have become, what shall I become still in the frightful agonies which await me, and in the incredible situation to which I am reduced for the rest of my life, if, remaining without an asylum where

I could escape my implacable persecutors, without compensation for the opprobrium which they made me suffer in this world, and without hope of ever obtaining the justice which is my due, I saw myself given over to the most horrible fate which any mortal has endured on the earth ? On the other hand, tranquil in my innocence, I did not imagine anything but esteem and benevolence for myself amongst men; and while my open and confiding heart poured itself out with friends and brothers, traitors surrounded me in silence, with nets forged in the depths of hell. Surprised by the most unforeseen of all evils, and the most terrible for a proud soul, dragged into the mud without ever knowing by whom nor wherefore, plunged into an abyss of ignominy, surrounded by horrible darkness across which I did not perceive aught but sinister objects, at my first surprise I was overwhelmed; and never should I have recovered from the discouragement in which this unforeseen class of misfortunes threw me, if I had not reserved in advance some strength to raise me up from my falls.

It was not until after years of agitation that, recovering finally my spirits, and beginning to return to myself, I knew the value of the resources which I had reserved for adversity. Decided upon all things of which it was necessary for me to judge, I saw on comparing my maxims to my situation that I was giving to the senseless judgments of men and to the small events of this brief life much more importance than they merited;

that this life was nothing but a state of trial—it mattered little that these trials were of such or such a sort, provided that there occurred the result for which they were destined, and that, in consequence, the more the trials were great, strong, multiplied, the more it was advantageous to know how to endure them. All the keenest sufferings lose their force for whoever sees in them a great and sure compensation; and the certainty of this compensation was the principal fruit that I drew from my preceding meditations.

It is true that in the midst of outrages without number and indignities without bounds by which I felt myself attacked on all sides, intervals of inquietude and doubt came, from time to time, to shake my hope and trouble my tranquillity. The powerful objections which I had not been able to resolve presented themselves thus to my spirit with the more force, to achieve my overthrow precisely at the moments when, overcharged with the weight of my destiny, I was ready to fall into discouragement; often new arguments, which I was able to form, returned into my spirit to aid those which had already tormented me. Ah! said I then in torments of heart ready to stifle me, who will guarantee me from despair if, in the horror of my lot, I do not see anything but delusions in the consolations which my reason furnishes me; if, destroying so its own work, it reverses all the support of hope and confidence which it has granted to me in adversity ? What support can illusions offer which do not console any but myself in this world? The whole present generation does not see anything but errors and prejudices in the sentiments by which I nourish myself: it finds truth and evidence in the system contrary to mine: it seems even not to believe that I have adopted it in good faith; and I myself in yielding to it with all my will have found insurmountable difficulties which it is impossible for me to resolve and which do not prevent me from persisting in it. Am I then alone wise, alone enlightened amongst mortals? to believe that things are so, suffices it that they are to my liking? Can I take an enlightened confidence in appearances which have nothing solid in the eyes of men, and which seem to me illusory to myself if my heart does not uphold my reason? Would it not be better to fight my persecutors with equal weapons by adopting their maxims than to remain under the delusion of mine as a prey of their attempts, without acting so as to cast them off? I believe myself wise, and I am nothing but dupe, victim, and martyr of a vain error.

How many times, in moments of doubt and uncertainty, I was ready to abandon myself to despair! If ever I had passed in this state a whole month, it would have been the end of my life and of myself. But these crises, though for the rest sufficiently common, have always been short; and now though I am not yet entirely delivered, they are so rare and so rapid, that they have not the power to trouble my rest. They are light troubles which do not affect my soul any more than a feather falling into a river can alter the course of the ſtream. I have felt that to re-argue the same points, upon which I had already decided, was to suppose for myself new illumination, or a more formed judgment, or more zeal for truth than I had at the time of my researches; that since not one of these cases was capable of being mine, I could not prefer, by any solid reason, opinions which, in the overthrow of despair, did not attack me except to augment my misery, to sentiments adopted in the vigour of age, in all the maturity of spirit, after the moſt careful examination, and in times when the calm of my life did not leave one other dominant intereſt than that of knowing the truth. To-day when my heart is wrung with diſtress, my soul worn out with ennui, my imagination upset, my mind troubled with so many frightful myſteries with which I am environed; to-day when all my faculties, weakened by old age and pain, have loſt all their vigour, shall I go about to deprive myself at pleasure of all the resources which I have reserved, and give more confidence to my declining reason in order to render myself unjuſtly unhappy, than to my full and vigorous reason in order to compensate me for the ills which I suffer without meriting them ? No; I am not either more wise, nor better disposed, nor of better faith than when I decided upon these great queſtions: I did not ignore, then, the difficulties with which I let myself be troubled to-day; they did not ſtop me, and if there have been presented some new ones of which I was not then aware, these are sophisms of a subtle metaphysic, which cannot balance the eternal truths admitted from all time, by all the sages, recognised by all nations, and graved on the human heart in ineffaceable letters. I know, in meditating on these matters, that the human understanding, circumscribed in all respects, cannot embrace them in all their extent; I hold, then, to that which is within my faculty, without engaging myself in that which surpasses it. This choice was reasonable; I embraced it formerly, and held to it with the assent of my heart and my reason. Upon what foundation should I renounce it to-day when so many powerful motives should hold me attached ? What danger do I see in following it ? What profit do I find in abandoning it ? In taking up the doctrine of my persecutors, should I take on also their morale, this morale without root and without fruit, which they spread out pompously in their books or in some glittering action on the stage, wherein nothing penetrates into the heart or the reason, or should I take on that other morale, secret and cruel, an interior doctrine of all their initiates, to which the other does not serve except as a mask, which they follow alone in their conduct, and which they have so skilfully practised in my respect ? This morale, purely offensive, does not serve for defence, and is not good except for aggression. How could it serve me in the state to which they have reduced me ? My innocence alone upholds me in my sorrows; and how much would I render myself still more unhappy, if depriving myself of this unique but powerful resource I substituted maliciousness for it ? Should I surpass them in the art of doing injury ? And when I had succeeded, of what ill would that which I could do them relieve me ? I should lose my own esteem, and I should gain nothing in place of it.

It is thus that, reasoning with myself, I succeeded in not letting myself be any more shaken in my principles by captious arguments, by insoluble objections, and by difficulties which pass the bounds of my comprehension, and perhaps that of the human mind itself. Mine, resting on the most solid basis that I could have given it, accustomed itself so well to remaining under the protection of my conscience, that no strange doctrine, old or new, could move it, nor trouble for a moment my repose. Fallen into languor and heaviness of spirit, I have forgotten even the reasonings upon which I founded my belief and my maxims: but I shall not ever forget the conclusions which I have drawn from them with the approbation of my conscience and my reason, and I hold to them henceforward. Let all the philosophers come to argue against them; they will lose their time and their trouble: I remain for the rest of my life, in everything, on the side which I took when I was best in a position to make a right choice.

Tranquil in these arrangements, I have found, with the agreement of myself, the hope and the consolation which I need in my situation: it is not possible that a solitude so complete, so permanent, so sad in itself, the ever perceptible and active animosity of the whole of the present generation, the indignities with which it overwhelms me without ceasing, do not cast me down sometimes into despair; hope shaken, discouraging doubts return from time to time to trouble my soul and fill it with sadness. It is then that, incapable of the operations of the mind, necessary to reassure myself, I need to recall my former resolutions; the cares, the attention, the sincerity of heart, that I have put into taking them, return to my memory, and give me back all my confidence. I refuse to give myself to all new ideas as to evil errors, which have only a false appearance, and are useless except to trouble my repose.

Thus held in the narrow sphere of my former knowledge, I have not, like Solon, the pleasure of being able to learn each day as I grow older, and I ought even to keep myself from the dangerous pride of wishing to grasp that which I am henceforward in no condition to know well. But if there remain for me few acquisitions to hope for on the side of useful knowledge, there remain very important ones to make on the side of the virtues necessary to my state; it is there that I shall have time to enrich and to ornament my soul with an acquisition which it can carry away with itself. When, delivered from this body which offends and blinds it, and seeing the truth unveiled, it perceives the vanity of all that knowledge of which our false wise men are so vain, it will bewail the moments wasted in this life in trying to acquire them. But patience, sweetness, resignation, integrity, impartial justice, are good which we carry about with ourselves, and with which we can be enriched without ceasing, without fearing that death itself can make us lose the prize: it is to this unique and useful study that I have consecrated the rest of my old age. Happy if, by progressing upon myself, I learn to leave life not better, because that is not possible, but more virtuous than I have entered it !

FOURTH PROMENADE

IN the small number of books which I still read
sometimes, Plutarch is the one which attracts me
and profits me the most. This was the first reading
of my childhood, it will be the last of my old age: he
is almost the only author which I have never read
without profit to myself. Day before yesterday, I
read in his Moral Essays the treatise " How One
Can Obtain Profit from One's Enemies." The same
day, in arranging certain pamphlets which have been
sent me by the authors, I fell on one of the journals
of the Abbé Royou, to the title of which he had put
these words: "Vitam vero impendenti,[1] Royou." Too
much aware of the turns of phrase of these gentlemen
to be moved by this, I understood that he had meant,
under this air of politeness, to tell me a cruel counter-
truth; but founded upon what ? Wherefore this
sarcasm ? What subject could I have given him there ?
To put into profit the lessons of the good Plutarch, I
resolved to employ the promenade of the next day in
examining myself upon deceitfulness, and I came to
this examination already confirmed in the opinion
taken that the " Know thyself " of the Temple of

[1] Life truly expended.

78

Delphi was not a maxim so easy to follow as I had believed in my " Confessions."

The next day, having made myself ready to execute this resolve, the first idea that came to me on beginning to meditate, was that of a piece of frightful deceit done in my early youth,[1] the memory of which has troubled me all my life, and comes, even in my old age, to sadden my heart, already broken in so many other ways. This deceit, which was a great crime in itself, must have been an even greater one by its effects which I have never known, but which remorse has made me suppose as cruel as possible. However, merely considering the state of mind in which I was in doing it, this deceit was nothing but a fruit of false shame; and very far from its starting as an intention to work harm on her who was the victim, I can swear in the face of Heaven that at the same instant when this unconquerable shame drove me towards it, I would have given all my blood with joy to turn the effect of it upon myself alone; it was a delirium which I cannot explain except by saying, as I believed I felt it, that in this instant my natural timidity overcame all the desires of my heart.

The remembrance of this unhappy act, and the inextinguishable regrets which it left me, have inspired me with a horror for deceit which has preserved my heart from this vice for the rest of my life. When I took my

---

[1] Rousseau is here referring to the episode of the servant girl Marion and the theft of a ribbon, narrated in Book II of the " Confessions."

motto, I felt myself made to merit it, and I did not doubt that I was worthy of it, when, at the remark of the Abbé Royou, I commenced to examine myself more seriously.

Then, in analysing myself with more care, I was very much surprised with the number of things of my own invention which I remember having declared as true in the time when, proud in myself of my love for truth, I sacrificed to it my safety, my interests, my person, with an impartiality of which I know no other example amid men.

What surprised me the most was that in recalling to myself these fabrications, I did not feel any true repentance. I whose horror for falsehood has nothing in my heart which balances it, I who would brave the scaffold if it could only be avoided by an act of deceit, by what strange inconsequence did I lie thus in gaiety of heart without need, without profit; and by what inconceivable contradiction did I not feel the least regret, I whom the remorse of a deceit has not ceased to afflict for fifty years ? I was never hardened to my faults; the moral instinct has always conducted me, my conscience has kept its first integrity; and even if it should be altered by bending to my interests, how, retaining all its uprightness on the occasions when man, forced by his passions, could at least excuse himself on the grounds of weakness, should it be lost only in indifferent matters when one has no excuse for vice ? I saw that the solution of this problem depends on the precision of judgment that I have to make in this point upon myself; and after having well examined it, here is the way in which I succeeded in explaining it to myself.

I remember having read in a philosophical book that to lie is to conceal a truth that one should display. It follows from this definition that to be silent about a truth that one is not obliged to speak is not to lie; but he who, not content in such a case to conceal the truth, says the contrary, does he lie or does he not lie ? According to the definition, one cannot say that he lies; because if he gives false money to a man to whom he owes nothing, he deceives this man without doubt, but he does not rob him.

There occur here two questions to examine, the one and the other very important—the first, when and how one owes truth to another, because one does not always owe it; the second, if there is a case in which one can innocently deceive. This second question is very often decided, I know well; negatively in books, where the most austere morality costs nothing to the author; affirmatively in society, where the morality of books passes for a chatter impossible to practice. Let me leave, then, these authorities which contradict themselves, and let me seek, by my own principles, to resolve these questions for myself.

General and abstract truth is the most precious of all goods: without it man is blind; it is the eye of reason. It is through this that man learns to conduct himself, to be that which he should be, to do that which he should do, to tend towards his true end. Particular and individual truth is not always a good; it is sometimes an evil, very often an indifferent thing. The things which it imports a man to know, and of which the knowledge is necessary to his happiness, are not perhaps in great number; but in whatever number they are, they are a good which belongs to him, which he has the right to reclaim wherever he finds it, and of which he cannot be deprived without committing the most iniquitous of all robberies, because this good is of the nature of a good common to all, to communicate which does not deprive the giver of that which he gives.

As for the truths which have no sort of utility, neither for instruction, nor for practice, how should they be an owed good, since they are not even a good? And since property is only founded upon utility, where there is no possible point of utility, there cannot be property. One can reclaim a piece of land however sterile, because one can at least inhabit the ground: but that a useless fact, unimportant in all respects and without value for anyone, should be true or false, does not interest anyone. In the moral order nothing is useless, any more than in the physical order; nothing can be due of that which is not good for anything: that a thing should be due, it is necessary that it is or may be useful. Thus the truth that is due is that which interests justice; and it is to profane the sacred name of truth to apply it to vain things the existence of which is indifferent to all, and the knowledge of which is useless for everything. Truth, deprived of every species of possible utility, cannot be a thing due, and in consequence he who is silent about it, or disguises it, does not lie.

But are there any truths so perfectly sterile that they are in every respect useless to all? This is another matter to discuss, and to which I shall return immediately. For the present, let us pass to the second question.

Not to say that which is true, and to say that which is false, are two very different things, but from which the same effect can nevertheless result, because this result is assuredly the same every time that the effect is null. Wherever truth is indifferent, the contrary error is indifferent also: whence it follows that in the same case he who deceives in speaking the contrary of truth is no more unjust than he who deceives in not declaring it; because, in the matter of useless truths, error has nothing worse about it than ignorance. That I believe the sand which is at the bottom of the sea to be white or red, does not matter to me more than not knowing what colour it is. How could one be unjust in not injuring anyone, because injustice only consists in the wrong done to another?

But these questions, so summarily decided, cannot furnish me with any sure application in practice, without many preliminary explanations necessary to

make with justice this application in all the cases
which may present themselves; because if the obligation to speak the truth is only founded upon its
utility, how should I constitute myself judge of this
utility? Very often the advantage of the one makes
for the prejudice of the other; private interest is
almost always in opposition to public interest. How
should one conduct oneself in such a case? Is it
necessary to sacrifice the utility of the absent person
to that of the person who is speaking? Is it necessary
to keep silent or to say the truth, that, profiting the one,
hurts the other? Is it necessary to weigh all that
one can say in the unique balance of the public good,
or in that of distributive justice? And am I assured
of knowing sufficiently all the relationships of things
so as not to expend the knowledge I dispose of except
according to the rules of equity? What is more, in
examining that which one owes to others, have I
sufficiently examined that which one owes to oneself,
that which one owes to truth for its own sake? If I
do no harm to another in deceiving him, does it follow
that I do no harm to myself, and does it suffice never
to be unjust in order to be always innocent?

What an embarrassing discussion, of which it would
be easy to extricate oneself by saying: Let us be always
true at the risk of everything that might result. Justice
itself is in the truth of things; deceit is always iniquity,
error is always imposture, when one gives that which
is not for the rule of that which one should do or

believe; and whatever effect results from the truth, one is always blameless when one has said it, because one has put nothing of one's own to it.

But this is to cut the question short, rather than to resolve it: we are not concerned with pronouncing whether it is good always to speak the truth, but whether it is always equally obligatory to speak it; and according to the definition of truth which I have examined, supposing that the answer is negative, to distinguish the cases when truth is rigorously due from those in which one may be silent without injustice, and disguise it without deceit; because I have found that such cases really exist. What concerns us is, then, to seek a sure rule to know these cases and to determine them.

But whence shall we draw such a rule, and the proof of its infallibility? In all questions of morality as difficult as this, I have always found the way to resolve them by the dictation of my conscience, rather than by the lights of my reason; never has the moral instinct deceived me; it has retained up to now this purity in my heart sufficiently for me to yield myself to it: and if it is silent sometimes in face of my passions in my conduct, it resumes its power over them in my memory; it is there that I judge myself with perhaps as much severity as I shall be judged by the sovereign Judge after this life.

To judge of the speeches of men by the effects they produce is often to appreciate them wrongly. Apart from the fact that these effects are not always felt and easy to understand, they vary as infinitely as the circumstances in which the discourses are held; but it is solely the intention of him who holds them that gives them value and determines their degree of malice or good will.   To speak falsely is not to lie except from the intention of deceiving, and the intention itself of deceiving, far from being always joined with that of injuring, has often a goal entirely contrary; but to render a deceit innocent it does not suffice that the intention of injuring should not be deliberate, it is necessary as well that the error into which one casts those to whom one speaks cannot injure them or anyone, in any way whatever.   It is rare and difficult to have this certainty; thus it is difficult and rare that a deceit should be perfectly innocent.   To lie for one's own advantage is imposture, to lie for the advantage of another is fraud, to lie in order to do harm is calumny —it is the worst kind of deceit: to lie without profit or prejudice to oneself or another is not to lie; it is not a deceit, it is fiction.

The fictions which have a moral object are called apologues or fables; and as their object is not or should not be anything except to envelop useful truths under sensible and agreeable forms, in such a case one does not attempt to hide the deceit of fact, which is nothing but the habit of truth; and he who puts forth a fable only as a fable does not lie in any fashion.

There are other fictions purely useless, such as the greater part of novels and romances, which, without containing any true instruction, have no object but amusement. These, deprived of all moral utility, cannot be estimated except by considering the intention of him who invented them; and when he brings them out affirming them to be real truths, one can scarcely affirm that these are not real deceits. Nevertheless, who has ever made a great point of such deceits, and who has made a serious reproach to those who create them? If there is, for instance, any moral object in the "Temple of Cnidus,"[1] this object is entirely obscured and spoilt by voluptuous details and lascivious images. What has the author done to cover these with a varnish of modesty? He has pretended that his work was the translation of a Greek manuscript, and he has told the story of the discovery of this manuscript in the way most likely to persuade his readers of the truth of his recital. If this is not a positive piece of deceit, let someone tell me what is lying? Nevertheless, who is there who has decided to make a crime of this deceit in the author, and to treat him on this account as an impostor?

One may say in vain that all this is only a pleasantry; that the author, in affirming his work to be a translation, has not wished to persuade anyone; that he has not persuaded anyone in fact, and that the public has not doubted for a moment that he was the author of the supposed Greek work of which he claimed to be the translator. I shall reply that such a pleasantry

---

[1] By Montesquieu.

without any object could be nothing but a foolish piece of childishness; that a liar does not lie less when he affirms, although he does not persuade; that it is necessary to detach from the instructed public the multitudes of simple and credulous readers upon whom the history of the manuscript, told by a serious author with an air of good faith, has really imposed, and who have drunken without fear, in a cup of ancient form, the poison which they would be at least on their guard against if it were presented in a modern vase.

That these distinctions be found or not in books, they are none the less made in the heart of every man who acts in accordance with good faith, who does not permit himself anything of which his conscience can reproach him; because to say a false thing to one's own advantage is not less to lie than if one said it to the prejudice of another, although the deceit is less criminal. To give the advantage to whoever ought not to have it is to disturb the order of justice; to attribute falsely to oneself or to another an act from which praise or blame, inculpation or disculpation may result is to do an unjust thing: hence all that which, contrary to the truth, injures justice in any fashion whatever is a deceit. This is the exact limit: but all that which, contrary to truth, does not interest justice in any way is nothing but a fiction, and I declare that whoever reproaches himself for a pure fiction as a deceit has a conscience more delicate than I.

That which one calls deceits are true deceits, because

to impose them either to the advantage of another, or to one's own, is not less unjuſt than to impose them to one's detriment; whoever praises or blames contrary to truth lies as soon as it concerns a real being. If a man is discussing an imaginary being, he can say all that he wishes without lying, at leaſt so far as he does not judge of the morality of the faƈts which he is inventing, and so far as he does not judge falsely; for then if he does not lie in faƈt, he lies againſt the moral truth, a hundred times more respeƈtable than that of faƈts.

I have seen some of those people whom are called truthful in the world; all their veracity was exhauſted in tedious conversations which faithfully cited the places, the times, the people; who did not permit themselves any fiƈtion, or to embroider upon any circumſtance, and who exaggerated nothing. In all that did not touch upon their intereſt, they were of the moſt inviolable fidelity in their narrations: but if it was a queſtion of treating some matter which concerned them, to narrate some faƈt which touched them, nearly all the colours were employed to present things under the light which was moſt advantageous; and if deceit is useful to them and they abſtain from speaking it themselves, they will favour it cleverly and behave in such a way that it is adopted without being imputed to them. So prudence commands: farewell to truth!

The man whom I call truthful does juſt the contrary. In perfeƈtly indifferent matters, the truth, which for the reſt the other man respeƈts so much, touches him very little, and he scarcely makes a scruple of amusing a company by controverted facts, from which there results no unjust judgment, neither for nor against whoever may be living or dead: but every discourse which produces for anyone profit or injury, esteem or dislike, praise or blame, against justice and truth, is a deceit which never shall approach his heart, or his mouth, or his pen. He is solidly truthful, even against his interest, although he troubles himself little about being so in idle conversation: he is truthful in that he does not seek to deceive anyone, that he is as faithful to the truth which accuses him as to that which honours him, and that he does not ever impose for his advantage, nor to injure his enemy. The difference, then, between my truthful man and the other is that he whom the world calls truthful is rigorously faithful to all truth which does not cost him anything, but not beyond that; while the man I call truthful never employs truth so faithfully as when it is necessary to immolate himself for her.

But, it may be said, how should one make this moral laxity accord with that ardent love for the truth with which I have glorified it? This love for truth then is false, because it suffers so much alloy? No; it is pure and true; but it is nothing but an emanation of the love of justice and does not ever desire to be false, although it may be often fabulous. Justice and truth are in such a man's spirit two synonymous words, which he takes indifferently one for another; the holy truth that his heart adores does not consist in indifferent facts and in useless names, but in rendering faithfully to each one whatever is owing to him in things that are inevitably his, in good or bad imputations, in retributions of honour or of blame, of praise or of disapproval; he is false neither against another, because his equity forbids and he does not wish to injure a person unjustly, nor for his own advantage, because his conscience forbids him, and he cannot appropriate what is not his own. It is above all of his own self-respect that he is watchful; this is the good which he can least afford to lose, and he would feel a real loss in acquiring that of others at the expense of this good. He lies, then, sometimes in indifferent matters without scruple and without thinking it a lie, never for the injury or for the profit of another or for himself: in all that depends upon historic truths, in all that concerns the conduct of men, or sociability, or useful knowledge, he will preserve both himself and others from error, as much as it depends upon him. Every deceit apart from this, according to him, is none. If the " Temple of Cnidus " is a useful work, the history of the Greek manuscript is nothing but a very innocent fiction; it is a deceit very punishable if the work is dangerous.

Such were my rules of conscience upon deceit and upon truth; my heart followed mechanically these rules before my reason had adopted them, and the moral instinct alone made the application. The criminal deceit of which poor Marion was the victim has left me with ineffaceable remorse, which has preserved me for the rest of my life not only from deceits of this kind, but from all those which, in whatever fashion they exist, might touch the interest and the reputation of another. In generalising thus upon the exclusion, I have dispensed myself from weighing exactly the advantage and the prejudice, and from marking the precise limits of the harmful deceit and of the officious deceit; in regarding the one and the other as culpable, I have forbidden myself both.

In this, as in all the rest, my temperament has had much influence upon my maxims, or rather upon my habits; because I have scarcely acted according to rule, or have scarcely followed other rules in anything except the impulses of my natural disposition. Never has a premeditated deceit approached my thought; never have I lied in my own interest; but often I have lied through shame in order to draw myself from embarrassment in indifferent matters, or matters which did not interest any but myself, when, having to sustain a discussion, the slowness of my ideas and the dryness of my conversation forced me to have recourse to fictions in order to say something. When it was necessary to speak and when amusing truths did not present themselves swiftly enough to my spirit, I made up fables in order not to remain silent: but in the invention of these fables I took care, as much as I could, that they should not be deceits; that is to say, that they did not wound either justice or truth, and that they were only fictions indifferent to all the world and to myself. My desire was entirely to substitute at least for the truth of facts a moral truth, that is to say to represent well the affections natural to the human heart, and to make some useful instruction always emerge—to make, in a word, moral stories, apologues; but there needed more presence of mind than I have, and more facility in words, to know how to put to profit, for instruction, the babble of talk. Its progress, more rapid than that of my ideas, forcing me almost always to speak before thinking, has often suggested to me foolish things and ineptitudes of which my reason disapproved, and which my heart disavowed at the moment they escaped from my mouth, but which, preceding my own judgment, could not be reformed by its censure.

It is still by this first and irresistible impulse of my temperament, that in unforeseen and rapid moments, shame and timidity have often extorted from me deceits in which my will took no part, but which preceded it in some fashion by the necessity of responding upon the moment. The profound impression of the memory of poor Marion may well make me refrain from all those deceits that might be of harm to others, but not from those that might serve to draw me from embarrassment when it concerns myself alone— which is not less against my conscience and my principles than those deceits which might influence the lot of another.

I call the Heavens to witness that if I could the

moment after retract the deceit which excuses me, and say the truth which weighs upon me, without making a new insult by withdrawing it, I would do it with a good heart; but the shame of being taken thus myself at fault holds me still back, and I repent very sincerely of my fault, without nevertheless being able to make reparation. An example will explain better what I wish to say, and show that I lie neither through interest nor through self-love, even less from envy or from malignity, but solely through embarrassment and shame, knowing very well sometimes that this deceit is known as such, and cannot serve me at all.

Some time ago, Monsieur F. asked me, against my custom, to go with my wife to dine, in a sort of picnic, with him and Monsieur B. at the house of Mrs. Blank, the proprietor of a restaurant, who with her two daughters would also dine with us. In the midst of the dinner, the eldest who had married some time ago, and was pregnant, decided to ask me, fixing her eyes upon me, if I had had children. I responded while blushing up to the eyes, that I had not had this happiness. She smiled maliciously and looked at the company: all this was not obscure, even for me.

It is clear at once that this response is not that which I should have wished to make; even if I should have had the intention of imposing it; because in the state of mind in which I saw the guests, I was sure that my response did not change anything in respect to their opinion on that point. They expected this negative, they provoked it even, to enjoy the pleasure of having made me lie.

I was not dolt enough to overlook this. Two minutes afterwards, the response that I should have made came to me of myself. " That is a very indiscreet question on the part of a young woman, to a man who has grown old as a bachelor." In speaking so, without lying, I should have put the laughers on my side, and I should have read a little lesson to them, which naturally would make them a little less impertinent in questioning me. I did nothing of all this, and I did not say what I should have said, I said what was not necessary to say, and what could not help me in any respect. It is certain, then, that neither my judgment nor my will dictated my response, and that it was the mechanical effort of my embarrassment. Otherwise, I should not have had this embarrassment, and I should have made the avowal of my faults with more freedom than shame, because I did not doubt that no one saw what redeemed them and what I felt within myself; but the eye of malignity upset and disconcerted me: in becoming more unhappy, I have become more timid, and never have I lied except through timidity.

I have never better felt my aversion for the lie than in writing my " Confessions "; because it is there that the temptations were frequent and strong, however little my inclination carried me in that direction; but far from having been silent about anything, dissimulated anything that was at my own expense, by a turn of mind that I have difficulty in explaining, and which comes perhaps from a dislike for all imitation, I felt myself rather drawn to lie in the contrary sense, and to accuse myself with too much severity rather than to excuse myself with too much indulgence; and my conscience assures me that one day I shall be judged less severely than I have judged myself. Yes, I say and I feel with a proud elevation of soul, in that book I have carried good faith, truth, frankness, as far, farther even (at least I believe) than any other man has done; knowing that the good surpassed the evil, I had an interest in saying everything, and I have said everything.

I have never said less; I have said more sometimes, not in the facts, but in the circumstances, and this species of deceit was more the effect of delirium of imagination than an act of will: I was wrong in calling it deceit, because none of these additions was one. I wrote my "Confessions" already old and disgusted with the vain pleasures of life that I had picked to pieces, and of which my heart had felt the void. I wrote them from memory; this memory failed me often or did not furnish me with anything but imperfect souvenirs, and I filled up the gaps with details which I imagined as a supplement to these memories, but which were never contradictory to them. I loved to expatiate on the happy moments of my life, and I embellished them sometimes with the ornaments with which tender regrets came to furnish me. I spoke of things which

FOURTH PROMENADE

I had forgotten as it seemed to me they should have been, as they had been perhaps in fact; never to the contrary of that which I recalled they had been. I lent sometimes strange charms to truth, but never have I put deceit in its stead in order to palliate my vices, or to arrogate virtues to myself.

And if sometimes, without thinking, by an involuntary movement, I have hidden the deformed side, in painting myself only in part as I was, these reticences have been compensated for by other reticences much more bizarre, which have often made me be silent about the good no less than the evil. This is a singularity of my natural temperament, which it is very pardonable in men not to believe, but which, unbelievable as it is, is not less real; I have often told the bad in all its baseness, I have rarely told the good in all its pleasantness, and often I have kept silent because it honoured me too much, and because, writing my "Confessions," I should have seemed to be eulogising myself. I have described my young years without priding myself upon qualities with which my heart was gifted, and even with the suppression of facts which made them too much in evidence. I here recall two facts of my early youth which both returned to my memory in writing them, but which I have rejected for the sole reason I have mentioned.

I went almost every Sunday to pass the day at Pâquis, at the house of M. Fazy, who had married one of my aunts, and who had there a factory of cotton prints. One day I was in the drying-house, in the room of the calendering machine, and I looked at the cylinders of lead; their shine pleased my eyes: I was tempted to touch them, and I stretched out my fingers to stroke the smooth side of the cylinder, when the young Fazy, having set himself at the wheel, gave it a half-turn so quickly that he did not take anything but the end of my two longest fingers, but this was enough to crush them at the end, and the two nails were torn out. I gave a piercing cry; Fazy stopped the wheel upon the instant; but the nails still remained between the cylinders, and the blood poured from my fingers. Fazy, frightened, cried out, left the wheel, embraced me, and begged me to hush my cries, adding that he was lost. In the midst of my pain, his own touched me; I was silent, we went to the carp-pond, where he helped me to wash my fingers and to staunch my blood with some moss. He begged me with tears not to accuse him; I promised and I kept my promise so well that twenty years after, no one knew by what adventure I had two of my fingers scarred; because they remained so always. I was kept in my bed more than three weeks, and for more than two months was unable to make use of my hand, saying always that a heavy stone, in falling, had crushed my fingers.

> " Magnanimous deceit! wherever is the true
> So fair, that it has power to conquer you ?"

This accident, however, was very deeply felt by me, under the circumstances, because it was the time of the military exercises, in which the townspeople took part, and we had formed a file of three other children of my age, with whom I was, in uniform, to do the exercises with the company of my quarter. I had the misfortune of hearing the drum of the company beating under my window for my three comrades while I was still in bed.

My other story is similar, but relates to a later age.

I was playing at Mall, at Plain-Palais, with one of my comrades called Plince. We quarrelled in the game; we beat each other, and during the battle he gave me on the bare head a stroke of the mallet so well directed, that, if he had been stronger, he would have split my skull. I fell in an instant. I have never in my life seen an agitation equal to that of this poor boy, when he saw my blood running down through my hair. He believed that he had killed me. He leapt upon me, embraced me, squeezed me tightly while bursting into tears and uttering piercing cries. I embraced him also with all my strength, while weeping like him in a confused emotion, which was not without some sweetness. Finally he made it his duty to staunch my blood which continued to run down; and seeing that our two handkerchiefs did not suffice, he brought me into his mother's house, as she had a small garden nearby. This good woman almost fainted on seeing me in such a condition, but she retained enough strength to bandage me; and after having well washed my wound she applied lily flowers crushed up in brandy—an excellent salve for wounds, and very often used in my country. Her tears and those of her son pierced my heart to such an extent that for a long time I looked on her as my mother and on her son as my brother, up to the time that having lost sight of them both, I forgot them by degrees.

I kept the same secret about this accident as about the other, and a hundred others have happened to me of a similar nature in my life, of which I have not even attempted to speak in my " Confessions," so little did I seek for the art of commending the good that I felt in my own character. No; when I have spoken against the truth that was known to me, it was never except in indifferent matters, and more, either from the embarrassment of speaking, or from the pleasure of writing rather than from any motive of interest for myself, either to the advantage or the prejudice of another; and whoever will read my " Confessions " impartially, if ever that happens, will know that the avowals I have made are more humiliating, more painful to make than those of an evil even greater, but less shameful to speak about; and which I have not avowed because I did not commit it.

It follows from all these reflections that the profession of truth which I have made has its foundation more upon the sentiments of right and equity than in the reality of things, and that I have followed in practice the moral directions of my conscience rather than abstract notions of false and true. I have often spoken fables, but have rarely deceived outright. In following these principles, I have given much power over myself to others, but I have done no wrong to anyone whatever, and I have not attributed to myself more advantage than was due. It is only in this way, it seems to me, that the truth is a virtue. In every other respect, it is not for us aught but a metaphysical entity, from which there results neither good nor evil.

I do not feel, however, my heart sufficiently content with these distinctions to believe myself entirely fault-less. In weighing with so much care what I owe to others, have I examined enough what I owe to myself? If it is necessary to be just to another, it is necessary also to be true to oneself; that is the homage which the honest man owes to his own dignity. When the sterility of my conversation forced me to make up for it by innocent fictions, I was wrong, because it was not necessary, in order to amuse another, to debase my-self; and when led on by the pleasure of writing, I added invented ornaments to real things, I was still more wrong, because to ornament the truth with fables is in fact to disfigure it.

But that which renders me more inexcusable is the motto[1] or device which I chose. This motto obliged me more than any man to a stricter pro-fession of truth, and it did not suffice that I should sacrifice everywhere my interests and my inclinations,

[1] Here Rousseau is speaking of the motto he adopted for his "Confessions," which was "to show to his fellow-beings a man in all the truth of his nature."

it was necessary also to sacrifice my weakness and my natural timidity. It was necessary to have the courage and the force to be always truthful, in every case, and to see that there did not ever rise fictions or fables from a mouth or a pen which were particularly consecrated to the truth. That is what I should have said to myself in assuming this proud motto, and in repeating it to myself so long as I dared carry it. Never has falseness dictated to me my deceits, they all sprang from weakness; but that excuses me badly. With a weak soul one can at least preserve oneself from vice; but to dare to profess great virtues is to be arrogant and overbold.

Here are some reflections which probably would never have entered my mind, if the Abbé Royou had not suggested them to me. It is very late, doubtless, to make use of them: but it is not too late at least to repair my mistake and to make my will obey the rule; because that is henceforward all dependent on me. In this then, and in all similar matters, the maxim of Solon is applicable to all ages, and it is never too late to learn, even from one's enemies, to be wise, true, modest, and not to presume upon oneself.

FIFTH PROMENADE

OF all the homes where I have lived (and I have had charming ones) none has made me so truly happy and has left me such tender regrets as the island of St. Peter, in the midst of the Lake of Bienne. This little island, which is called at Neufchâtel the island of La Motte, is scarcely known, even in Switzerland. No traveller, so far as I am aware, has made mention of it. However, it is very agreeable, and singularly situated for the happiness of a man who loves to limit himself; for, although I am perhaps the only man to whom his destiny has made this a law, I cannot believe that I am the only one who has a taste so natural, although I have not found it up to now in anyone else.

The shores of the Lake of Bienne are wilder and more romantic than those of the Lake of Geneva, because the rocks and the woods surround the water more closely; but they are not less smiling. If there is less cultivation of fields and vines, fewer houses and woods, there are also more natural greenery, more meadows, more haunts shaded with coppices, more frequent contrasts and undulations of ground close together. As there are not, upon these happy shores, comfortable main roads for carriages, the country is little frequented

by travellers; but it is interesting for those solitary con-
templatives who love to intoxicate themselves at leisure
with the charms of nature, and to meditate in a silence
disturbed by no sound except the cry of the eagles,
the occasional twittering of birds, and the rolling down
of torrents which fall from the mountain. This
beautiful basin, with a form almost round, contains
two little islands in its midst, the one inhabited and
cultivated, of about a half-league in circuit; the other,
more small, desert and fallow, which will be destroyed
in the end by the transportations of earth which are
being carried on incessantly in order to repair the
damages which the waves and the storms make to the
greater. It is thus that the substance of the weak is
always employed to the profit of the powerful.

There is only a single house on the island, but large,
agreeable and comfortable, which belongs to the
hospital at Berne, as does the island; there a comptroller lives with his family and domestics. It contains
a large farm-yard, a pigeon-house, and reservoirs for
fish. The island, in its small compass, is so varied in
its fields and aspects, that it offers all sorts of sites and
allows all sorts of cultivation. One finds there fields,
vines, woods, fat pastures shaded with woods, and
bordered with small trees of every species, which
are kept fresh by the proximity of the water; a high
terrace, planted with two rows of trees, borders the
island in its length, and in the midst of this terrace
has been built a fine hall, where the inhabitants of the

neighbouring banks gather together and dance on Sundays during the vintage season.

It is in this island that I took refuge after the ſtoning of Motiers. I found the sojourn so charming, I carried on a life so suitable to my humour, that resolved to finish my days there, I had no other disquiet except that I might not be allowed to carry out this plan, which did not accord with that of going to England, of which I already felt the firſt effeċts. In the presentiments which disquieted me, I could have wished that this asylum had been made a perpetual prison, that I had been confined there for the whole of my life, and that by taking from me all power and every hope to leave, I had been forbidden every sort of communication with the mainland, in such a way that ignorant of all that was being done in the world I could have forgotten its exiſtence, and that the world could have forgotten mine also.

I was allowed to pass only two months in this island, but I could have passed there two years, two centuries, and the whole of eternity, without being weary one moment, although I had not, with my wife, other society than that of the receiver, of his wife, and of his servants, who all were in truth very good people, and nothing more; but that was precisely what I needed. I count these two months as the happieſt time of my life, and so happy, that it would have sufficed me throughout life, without for a single moment allowing in my soul the desire for a different ſtate.

What then was this happiness, and in what did its enjoyment consist ?   I shall let it be guessed at by all the men of this century, from the description of the life which I led there.   A delicious idleness was the first and the principal enjoyment that I wished to taste in all its sweetness; and all that I did during my stay was nothing but the charming and necessary occupation of a man who is vowed to idleness.

The hope that the Government would not ask more than to leave me in this isolated place where I was entwined by myself, which it was impossible for me to leave without assistance and without being seen, and where I could have neither communication nor correspondence except by the help of the people who surrounded me; that hope, I say, gave me the further hope of finishing my days more quietly than I had passed them; and the idea that I should have the time to arrange my life at leisure made me commence by having no arrangement at all.   Transported there suddenly, alone and unprovided for, I sent successively for my wife, my books, and my little luggage, which I had the pleasure of not unlocking, leaving my chests and my trunks as they had arrived and living in the home where I counted upon finishing my days, as in an inn whence I should depart on the morrow.   All things, as they were, went so well that to wish to arrange things better was to spoil them.   One of my greatest delights was above all to leave my books well boxed up, and not to have a writing-desk.   When unlucky

letters made me take up the pen to answer, I borrowed
with murmurs the writing-pad of the comptroller,
and I hastened to return it, in the vain hope of having no need to reborrow it. In place of sad paper-
heaps and all that book trade, I filled my room with
flowers and seeds; because I was then in the first
fervour of my botanising, for which the doctor of In-
vernois had inspired in me a taste which soon became a
passion. Since I did not wish to work any more at writing, there was necessary for me an amusement which
pleased me, and which gave me no more trouble than
that which a lazy man cares to give. I undertook to
make the Flora of St. Peter's Island, and to describe
all the plants there, without omitting one, in sufficient
detail to occupy me for the rest of my days. They
say that a German has written a book on lemon-peel;
I would have done one on each grain of the fields, on
every moss of the wood, on each lichen which carpets
the rocks; finally I did not want to leave a blade of
grass, a vegetable atom which was not fully described.
In consequence of this fine project, every morning
after breakfast, which we took together, I went, a
magnifying glass in hand, and my " System of Nature "
under my arm, to visit a portion of the island, which I
had for this purpose divided into small squares, with the
intention of going over them one after the other, in each
season. Nothing is more singular than the ravishments,
the ecstasies which I felt at each observation I had
made upon the structure and the vegetable organisa-

tion, and upon the play of the sexual parts in the fructification, of which the system was then altogether new to me. The distinction of generic characters, of which I had not beforehand the least notion, enchanted me as I verified them in common species, while waiting till rarer varieties were offered to me. The forking of the two long stamens of the self-heal, the springing of those of the nettle and the wallflower, the bursting of the fruit of the garden-balsam, and of the capsule of the box-bush, a thousand small tricks of fructification, which I observed for the first time, filled me with joy, and I went about asking people if they had seen the horns of the self-heal, as La Fontaine asked if people had read Habakkuk. At the end of two or three hours, I returned laden with an ample harvest, a provision of amusement for the afternoon at home, in case of rain. I spent the rest of the morning in going about with the comptroller, his wife and Thérèse, visiting their workmen and their harvest, often setting hand to the work with them; and often the Bernese who came to see me have found me in a tree, bound about with a sack which I filled with fruits, and which I let down afterwards to earth with a cord. The exercise which I had taken in the morning, and the good humour which is inseparable from it, made the repose of dining very agreeable; but when it was too long prolonged, and the fine weather invited me, I could not wait so long; and while the others were still at the table I escaped, and threw myself alone into a boat which

FIFTH PROMENADE

I rowed into the midſt of the lake, when the water was calm: and there, ſtretching myself out at full length in the boat, my eyes turned towards heaven, I let myself go and wander about slowly at the will of the water, sometimes during many hours, plunged into a thousand confused but delicious reveries, which, without having any well-determined objeƈt, nor con-ſtancy, did not fail to be in my opinion a hundred times preferable to all that I have found sweeteſt in what are called the pleasures of life. Often warned by the going down of the sun at the hour of sunset, I found myself so far away from the island, that I was forced to labour with all my strength to arrive before the night closed down. Other times, in place of letting myself drift about in the water, I pleased myself by skirting the green banks of the island, of which the limpid waters and the fresh umbrages have often tempted me to bathe in them. But one of my moſt frequent navigations was to go from the large to the small island, to disembark and to pass the afternoon, sometimes in very circumscribed promenades in the midſt of the thickets of shrubs of every species, and sometimes to eſtablish myself on the top of a sandy hillock, covered with fine grass, with wild thyme, with the flowers of the sanfoin, and with trefoil which apparently had been sown previously, and was very good to lodge rabbits, who could there multiply in peace, without fearing anything, and without harm-ing anything.

REVERIES OF A SOLITARY

I gave this idea to the comptroller, who brought from Neufchâtel male and female specimens, and we went in great state, his wife, one of her sisters, Thérèse and myself, to establish them in the small island, which they commenced to populate before my departure, and where they have prospered without a doubt, if they have been able to sustain the rigour of the winter. The founding of this small colony was a fête. The pilot of the Argonauts was not more proud than I, leading in triumph the company and the rabbits from the large to the small island; and I noted with pride that the wife of the comptroller, who feared the water excessively, and always felt ill upon it, embarked under my conduct with confidence, and did not display any fear during the crossing.

When the agitated lake did not permit me to navigate on it, I passed my afternoon in going over the island, botanising to right and left, seating myself now in the most pleasant and most solitary nooks, to dream at my ease, sometimes on terraces or mounds, to sweep with my eyes the superb and ravishing surroundings of the lake and its banks, crowned on one side by neighbouring mountains, and on the other, enlarged by rich and fertile plains, of which the view was extended to the blue mountains, more distant, which bounded the horizon.

When the evening approached, I descended from the summits of the island, and I went gladly to sit down on the border of the lake, on the shore, in some hidden nook: there, the sound of the waves and the agitation of the water, fixing my senses and driving every other agitation from my soul, plunged it into a delicious reverie, where the night often surprised me without my having perceived it. The flux and reflux of this water, its continuous sound, swelling at intervals, struck ceaselessly my ears and my eyes, responding to the internal movements which reverie extinguished in me, and sufficed to make me feel my existence with pleasure, without taking the trouble to think. From time to time was born some weak and brief reflection on the instability of earthly things, of which the surface of the water offered me the image; but soon these light impressions effaced themselves in the uniformity of continuous movement which rocked me, and which, without any active help from my soul, did not fail to attach me to such an extent that when summoned by the hour and the signal agreed upon, I could not tear away without an effort.

After supper, when the evening was beautiful, we all went together to make a tour of the walk on the terrace, to breathe the air of the lake and its freshness. We rested in the pavilion, we laughed, talked, sung some old song which was far better than modern discord, and finally went to rest content with the day, and not desiring anything but its like for the morning.

Such is, leaving to one side unforeseen and importunate visits, the manner in which I passed my time in this island, during the stay that I made there.

Let someone tell me now what there was so attractive to excite in my heart regrets so lively, so tender, and so durable, that at the end of fifteen years it is still impossible for me to think of this beloved habitation, without feeling myself every time still carried away by agitations of desire.

I have remarked in the vicissitudes of a long life that the epochs of the sweetest enjoyments and of the most lively pleasures are not in every case those of which the remembrance draws me and touches me most nearly. These short moments of delirium and of passion, however strong they may be, are nevertheless, by their vivacity itself, only scattered points in the line of life. They are too rare and too rapid to constitute a state; and the happiness which my heart regrets is not composed of fugitive instincts, but a simple and permanent state, which has nothing keen in itself, but the duration of which increases the charm, to the point of finding there the supreme felicity.

All is in a continuous flux upon earth. Nothing keeps a constant and fixed form, and our affections which attach themselves to exterior things pass away and change necessarily like them. Always in advance or behind us, they recall the past, which is no more, or presage the future, which often is not to be; there is nothing solid there to which the heart can attach itself. Therefore one has scarcely here below anything but passing pleasures; for the happiness which lasts, I doubt if it is known. Scarcely is there, in our most living delights, a moment where the heart can truly say to us: I wish that this moment should laſt forever. And how can one call that happiness which is a fugitive ſtate which leaves our heart unquiet and empty, which makes us regret something beforehand or desire something after?

But if there is a ſtate where the soul finds a position sufficiently solid to repose thereon, and to gather together all its being, without having need for recalling the paſt, nor to climb on into the future; where time counts for nothing, where the present laſts forever, without marking its duration in any way, and without any trace of succession, without any other sentiment of privation, neither of enjoyment, of pleasure nor pain, of desire nor of fear, than this alone of our exiſtence, and which this feeling alone can fill entirely: so long as this ſtate laſts, he who finds it may be called happy, not with an imperfeᑕ happiness, poor and relative, such as that which one finds in the pleasures of life, but with a sufficing happiness, perfeᑕ and full, which does not leave in the soul any void which it feels the need of filling. Such is the ſtate in which I found myself often at the island of St. Peter, in my solitary reveries, either reſting in my boat which I let drift at the will of the water, or seated on the banks of the agitated lake, or elsewhere at the border of a beautiful river, or of a brooklet murmuring on the sand.

What is the nature of one's enjoyment in such a situation? Nothing external to oneself, nothing except oneself and one's own existence; so long as this state lasts, one suffices to oneself, like God. The sentiment of existence, deprived of all other affection, is in itself a precious sentiment of contentment and of peace, which alone suffices to render this existence dear and sweet to whoever knows how to remove from himself all the sensual and terrestrial impressions which come unceasingly to distract us, and to trouble the sweetness here below. But the greater part of men agitated by continual passions know little of this state, and having tasted it but imperfectly for a few instants, do not retain anything but an obscure and confused idea, which does not permit them to feel the charm. It would not even be good in the present state of affairs, that avid of these sweet ecstasies, they should be disgusted with the active life, of which their needs always being reborn, prescribe to them the duty. But an unfortunate who has been withdrawn from human society, and who can do nothing here below that is useful or good for himself or for others, can find in this state consolations for all human enjoyments which fortune and men cannot remove from him.

It is true that these consolations cannot be felt by all souls, nor in all situations. It is necessary that the heart should be at peace and that no passion should come to trouble the charm. Certain dispositions on the part of the man who experiences them are necessary; it is also necessary in the gathering together of environing objects. There is needed neither an absolute repose nor too much agitation, but a uniform and moderate movement which should have neither shocks nor intervals. Without movement, life is only a lethargy. If the movement is unequal or too strong it awakens; in recalling us to environing objects, it destroys the charm of the reverie and draws us out of ourselves, to put us in an instant under the yoke of fortune and man and to bring us back to the feeling of our unhappiness. An absolute silence leads to sadness; it offers us an image of death; thus the help of a light-hearted imagination is necessary and presents itself naturally to those whom the heavens have gratified with it. The movement which does not come from without, then, is made within us. The repose is less, it is true; but it is also more agreeable when light and sweet ideas, without agitating the depths of the soul, do nothing but brush the surface. There is needed only enough of them to remember oneself while forgetting all one's evils. This species of reverie can be tasted everywhere where one can be tranquil; and I have often thought that at the Bastille, and even in a cell where no object would strike my sight, I could still have dreamed agreeably.

But it is necessary to admit that this was done better and more favourably in a fertile and solitary island, naturally circumscribed and separated from the rest of the world, where nothing offered itself to me but smiling images, where nothing recalled sad remembrances, where the society of the small number of inhabitants was binding and sweet, without being interesting up to the point of occupying me incessantly, where I could finally yield myself the whole day, without obstacles and without cares, to the occupations of my taste or to the softest idleness. The opportunity without a doubt was excellent for a dreamer, who knowing how to nourish himself with agreeable illusions, in the midst of the most displeasing objects, could recall them at ease while adding to them everything which actually struck his senses. On emerging from a long and sweet reverie, seeing myself surrounded with verdure, flowers, birds, and letting my eyes wander afar over romantic banks which bordered a vast extent of clear and crystalline water, I assimilated to my fictions all these amiable objects; and finding myself brought back by degrees to myself and to what surrounded me, I could not distinguish the point of separation between fiction and reality, so much did all concur equally to render dear the solitary and absorbed life that I lived in this fair dwelling. If it could only come again! and if I could only go and end my days in this dear island, without ever leaving it, or ever seeing any inhabitant of the continent who would recall to me the memory of the calamities of every sort which they have been pleased to heap upon me for so many years! They would be soon forgotten for ever; without a doubt they would not forget me in the same way; but what would this matter to me, provided that they had no access to me to trouble my repose? Delivered from all the terrestrial passions which the tumult of social life engenders, my soul would frequently leap above this atmosphere and have converse beforehand with the celestial intelligences, of which it hopes to augment the number in a short time. Mankind will take care, I know, not to give me back so sweet an asylum where they would not leave me. But they will not prevent me at least from transporting myself there every day upon the wings of the imagination, and from tasting during some hours the same pleasure as if I were still inhabiting it. That which I did there was to dream at my ease. In dreaming that I am there, do I not do the same thing? I do even more; to the attraction of an abstract and monotonous reverie, I join the charming images which vivify it. These objects often escape from my senses in my ecstasies; but now, the more my reverie is profound, the more strongly it paints them. I am often still in the midst of them, and more agreeably even than if I were actually so. The misfortune is, that to the degree in which my imagination becomes tepid, all this comes with more difficulty, and does not endure so long. Alas! it is when one commences to quit one's own carcase that one is the most offended by it!

SIXTH PROMENADE

WE have scarcely a mechanical movement of which we cannot find the cause in our own heart, if we know how to seek it there.

Yesterday, in passing down the new boulevard to look for plants along the Bièvre, in the direction of Gentilly, I made a bend to the right in approaching the Barrière d'Enfer; and turning off into the country, I went by the road to Fontainebleau, to reach the heights which border this little river. This walk was entirely indifferent in itself; but on recalling that I had made mechanically the same détour many times, I sought the cause of it in myself, and I could not prevent myself from laughing when I discovered it.

In the corner of the boulevard, at the exit of the Barrière d'Enfer, there was established every day in summer a woman who sold fruit, cordial, and little rolls. This woman had a small boy, very nice but lame, who, limping on his crutches, went about good-manneredly asking alms from the passers-by. I had struck up an acquaintance with this little fellow; he did not fail, every time I passed, to offer me his compliments, always followed by my little offering. At first, I was charmed to see him. I gave to him with a good heart, and I continued for some time to do this with

the same pleasure, joining even the pleasure of exciting
and listening to his small talk, which I found agreeable.
This pleasure, become by degrees a habit, found itself,
I know not why, transformed into a species of duty of
which I soon felt the weight, above all on account of
the preliminary harangue which it was necessary to
listen to, and in which he did not ever fail to often call
me M. Rousseau, in order to show that he knew me
well; which showed me sufficiently to the contrary that
he did not know me any more than those who had
instructed him.   From that time on, I passed by there
less willingly, and finally I acquired mechanically the
habit of making most frequently a détour when I
approached this traverse.

This is what I discovered on reflecting, because
nothing of all this had been offered up to that time
distinctly to my thought.   This observation recalled
to me successively multitudes of others, which have
confirmed me in thinking that the true and human
motives of the greater part of my actions are not so
clear to myself as I had long supposed: I know and I
feel that to do good is the truest happiness that the
human heart can taste; but for a long time, this happiness has been beyond my reach, and it is not in such a
miserable lot as mine that one can hope to effect with
joy and fruit a single truly good action.   The greatest
care of those who regulate my destiny has been to see
that nothing should exist for me except in false and
deceitful appearance, and so a motive of virtue is only

a lure which is offered to me to draw me into the trap where they wish to bind me fast. I know this; I know that the only good which is henceforth in my power to do is to abstain from acting, for fear of doing harm without wishing to do so and without knowing it.

But there were times more happy when, following the movements of my heart, I could sometimes make another heart content; and I owe myself the honourable witness that each time that I have been able to taste this pleasure, I have found it sweeter than any other; this inclination was strong, true, pure; and nothing, in my most secret heart, has ever denied it. Nevertheless, I have often felt the load of my own benefactions by the chain of duties which they brought with them: then the pleasure has disappeared, and I have not found, in the continuation of the same course which had charmed me beforehand, anything but an almost insupportable trouble. During my short prosperity, many people had recourse to me, and never in all the services that I could render them have any of them been rejected. But from these first acts of goodness, poured out with effusion of heart, were born chains of successive engagements that I had not foreseen, and of which I could no longer shake off the yoke: my first services were, in the eyes of those who received them, only the earnest of those which should follow; and as soon as some unfortunate had thrown me upon the hook of a benefit received, it was henceforward settled that this first benefaction, free and voluntary, should become an indefinite right to all those of which he could have need in the future, without even my inability to grant them being sufficient to free me.   That is how very sweet enjoyments were transformed for me in the sequel into onerous subjections.

These chains, however, did not appear to me very weighty, so long as I lived in obscurity unknown to the public; but when once my person was advertised by my writings (a grave fault without a doubt, but more than expiated by my woes), from that time on I became the general bureau to which all the sufferers or so-called sufferers addressed themselves, the butt of all the adventurers who sought for dupes, of all those who under the pretext of the great credit which they pretended to attribute to me, wished to take advantage of me in one way or another.   It is then that I had opportunity to observe that all the inclinations of nature, without excepting benevolence itself, when carried or followed out into society without prudence and without choice, change their nature and become often as harmful as they were useful in their first administration.   So many cruel exploitations little by little changed my first opinions, or rather, by closing them within their strict limits, taught me to follow less blindly my inclination to do good, when it only served to favour the wickedness of another.

But I have no regret for these experiences, because they have procured me through reflection new light upon the knowledge of myself and upon the true motives of my conduct in a thousand circumstances about which I have often deluded myself: I saw that, to do good with pleasure, it was necessary that I should act freely, without constraint, and that, to take from me all the sweetness of a good deed, it sufficed that it should become a duty for me. From thenceforward the weight of the obligation made sweetest pleasures a burden to me; and as I have said in "Émile," I think, I should have been a bad husband among the Turks at the hour when the public crier called them to fulfil the duties of their condition.

This is what has modified greatly the opinion that I had for a long time of my own virtue; because there is no virtue in following out one's own inclinations, and in giving oneself, when they carry us in that direction, the pleasure of doing good; but virtue consists in conquering them when duty commands us to do that which it prescribes us, and that is what I have known less how to do than any man in the world. Born sensitive and kindly, carrying pity to the point of weakness, and feeling my soul exalted by all that is akin to generosity, I was humane, benevolent, charitable from taste, from passion even, so long as my heart alone was concerned; I should have been the best and the kindest of men if I had been the most powerful, and in order to extinguish in me all desire of vengeance, it would have been enough to have the power to avenge myself. I could even have been just against my own interest without difficulty; but to act against the interest

of those who were dear to me I could not find resolution.
As soon as my duty and my heart were in contradiction,
the first rarely had the victory, unless it merely required
me to abstain: then I was most often strong; but to act
against my inclination was always impossible to me.
Whether it were men, or duty, or even necessity which
commanded me, when my heart was silent, my will
remained dumb, and I could not obey: I saw the evil
which menaced me, and I let it come rather than
disturb myself to anticipate it.   I commenced sometimes with effort; but this effort wearied and exhausted
me rapidly; I could not continue.   In every imaginable
thing, that which I did not do with pleasure was soon
impossible for me to do.

There is more: the constraint, in accordance with my
desire, sufficed to destroy it and to change it into
repugnance, even into aversion, whenever it acted too
strongly; and this is what renders painful the good
deeds which others demand of me, and which I should
do of myself if they were not demanded.   A purely
disinterested good deed is certainly a work which I love
to do; but when he who has received it makes it the
reason for exacting a continuation under threat of his
hatred, when he makes it a law that I should be for
ever his benefactor, for having in the first place taken
pleasure in being so, from thenceforward the trouble
increases and pleasure vanishes.   That which I do when
I yield is from weakness and shame; but good will does
not enter into it; and far from applauding myself, I

reproach myself in my own conscience for doing good grudgingly.

I know that there is a sort of contract, perhaps one of the most sacred, between the benefactor and the recipient; it is a sort of association that they form with each other, closer than that which unites men in general; and if the recipient engages himself tacitly to gratitude, the benefactor engages himself to keep in regard to the other, so long as he does not render himself unworthy, the same good will which he has just shown him, and it is his part to renew these acts every time he can when he is required to do so. These conditions are not expressly stated, but they are the natural effects of the relation which is established between the two parties. He who, for the first time, refuses a gratuitous service which someone asks him for, does not give any right of complaint to the person whom he has refused; but he who in a similar case refuses to the same man the same kindness which he has granted beforehand destroys a hope which he has given him reason to feel; he deceives and denies an expectation which he has caused to exist. In this refusal there is a feeling of more injustice and hardness than in the other; but it is not less the result of an independence dear to the heart, which it does not renounce without an effort. When I pay a debt, it is a duty that I fulfil. When I make a gift, it is a pleasure that I give myself. Now the pleasure of fulfilling one's duty is among those which the sole practice of virtue brings to birth: those which come to us immediately from nature do not raise themselves so high as this.

After so many sad experiences, I have learnt to foresee from a distance the consequences of my impulses carried out, and I have often abstained from a good act, which I wished to perform, and had the power to do, frightened at the subjection to which in the long run I was about to submit, if I yielded myself inconsiderately. I have not always felt this fear: on the contrary, in my youth, I attached myself to my own benefactions, and I have often felt similarly that those whom I obliged became fond of me through gratitude rather than through interest. But things completely changed, in this respect as in every other, as soon as my misfortunes began; I have lived since then in a new generation which did not resemble the former, and my own sentiments towards others have suffered from the changes which I found in their sentiments towards me. The same people that I have known in these two different generations have, so to speak, successively become like the rest: from being true and frank as they were at the start, they have become that which they are, they have done as all the others; and for the sole reason that the times have changed, men changed with them. How could I keep the same feelings towards those in whom I find the contrary of that which made these sentiments exist? I do not hate them because I cannot hate, but I cannot prevent myself from feeling the contempt they merit, nor abstain from making it known.

Perhaps, without perceiving it, I have changed myself more than I ought: what nature could resist without alteration in a situation akin to mine? Convinced by twenty years of experience that all the right inclinations which Nature placed in my heart have been turned by my destiny and by those who have control of it to the prejudice of myself or of others, I can no longer regard a good act which is offered to me to do, except as a snare which is held forth to me, and beneath which is hidden some evil. I know, whatever may be the effect of my act, that I shall none the less have the merit of my good intention: yes, this merit is there always, without a doubt, but the interior charm is no more there, and as soon as this stimulant is lacking to me I do not feel anything but indifference and coldness within myself: and sure that in place of doing an action truly useful I am only acting as a dupe; the indignation of self-respect, joined to the disavowal of reason, does not inspire me with anything but repugnance and resistance, when I should have been full of ardour and zeal in my natural condition.

There are kinds of adversity which elevate and strengthen the soul, but there are other kinds which cast it down and kill it: such is that of which I am the prey. If there had been a little bad leaven in my soul it would have been made to ferment to excess by adversity, and

would have rendered me frantic, but it has only made
me a nonentity. Incapable of well-doing both for
myself and for others, I have abstained from acting; and
this state, which is only innocent because it is forced,
has made me find a sort of sweetness in yielding myself
fully without reproach to my natural inclination. I
go too far, without doubt, because I evade oppor-
tunities of action, even where I do not see anything
but good to do; but, certain that I am not allowed to
see things as they are, I abstain from judging upon
the appearances which are given them; and with
whatsoever lure the motives of action are covered, it
suffices that these motives should be left within my
grasp for me to be sure that they are deceitful.

My destiny seems to have held forth, from my
childhood, the first snare which rendered me for a
long time so apt to fall into all others; I was born the
most confiding of men, and for forty years together
never was this confidence deceived for a single time.
Falling suddenly among another order of persons
and things, I slipped into a thousand snares without perceiving one of them; and twenty years of
experience have scarcely sufficed to enlighten me as
to my lot. Once convinced that there was nothing
but deceit and falsity in the grimacing demonstra-
tions which have been lavished upon me, I passed
rapidly to the other extreme; because, when we have
once departed from our natural disposition, there are
no bounds to restrain us. Thenceforward I have

been disgusted with men, and my will, concurring with theirs in this respect, held me still more remote from them than all their machinations.

Whatever they may do, this repugnance cannot ever reach aversion; in thinking of the dependence in which they have put themselves in order to hold me in theirs, they create in me a true pity; if I am unhappy, they are unhappy too, and every time that I return home, I find them always to be pitied. Pride perhaps is still mingled with these judgments; I feel myself too far above them to hate them; they can interest me at the most up to contempt, but never up to hatred; finally I love myself too much to be able to hate anyone that exists. This would be to enclose, to contract my existence; and I would rather spread it over the whole of the universe.

I would rather fly than hate them; their aspect strikes my senses, and through them, my heart, with impressions which a thousand cruel looks render painful to me; but the uneasiness ceases as soon as the object which has caused it has disappeared. Despite myself, I give my attention to them when they are present, but never to the remembrance of them; when I do not see them, they are for me as if they had never existed.

They are not even indifferent except in so far as concerns me; for, in their relations between each other, they can still interest and move me like the people of a drama which I see presented. My moral being would have to be destroyed for justice to become indifferent to me: the spectacle of injustice and of deceit still makes my blood boil with rage; the acts of virtue in which I do not see either make-believe or ostentation always make me quiver with joy and still draw forth my tears. But it is necessary that I should see them and appreciate them myself because, after my own experience, I should be senseless to adopt the judgment of men on any point, and to believe anything upon the faith of another.

If my face and my features were as perfectly unknown to men as my character and my natural disposition are, I could still live without pain in the midst of them; their society even might please me so long as I should be perfectly strange to them; yielding without constraint to my natural inclinations, I should love them still if they did not ever concern themselves with me. I should exercise upon them an universal benevolence and a perfectly disinterested one; but without ever forming any particular attraction and without wearing the yoke of any duty, I should do unto them, freely and of my own will, all that they have so much trouble to do when urged by their self-respect and constrained by all their laws.

If I had remained free, obscure, isolated, as I was made to be, I should have done nothing but good, because I have not the germ of any harmful passion in my heart; if I were invisible and powerful as God, I should have been beneficent and good like Him.

It is strength and liberty which make excellent men: weakness and slavery have made nothing but base ones. If I had been the possessor of the ring of Gyges, it would have drawn me from dependence upon men, and would have put them into dependence upon me. I have often asked, in my day-dreams, what use I should have made of this ring; because it is there that the temptation of abusing it must be near to power. Able to content my desires, and to do anything, without being able to be deceived by anyone, what could I have desired continually ? One simple thing: that would be to see all hearts contented; the sight of public felicity could alone have touched my heart with a permanent sentiment, and the ardent desire of helping it would have been my most constant passion. Always just without partiality, and always good without weakness, I should have equally preserved myself from blind suspicion and implacable hatred, because seeing men as they are, and reading easily the very depths of their hearts, I should have found very few sufficiently amiable to meet all my affections, very few sufficiently odious to merit all my hatred, and their deceitfulness even would have disposed me to pity them, by the certain knowledge of evil which they do to themselves in trying to do it to others. Perhaps, in moments of gaiety, I should have been childish enough sometimes to work miracles; but perfectly disinterested for myself, and having nothing but my natural inclinations for law, for each act of severe justice, I should have performed a thousand of clemency and equity; a minister of Providence, and a dispenser of its laws, according to my power, I should have performed miracles wiser and more useful than those of the Golden Legend and of the tomb of St. Médard.

There is but one point upon which the faculty of penetrating everywhere invisible might have made me seek temptations to which I should have ill resisted; and once entered into these ways of straying, where should I not have been conducted by them ? It would be to know ill both nature and myself, to flatter myself that these facilities would not have seduced me, or that reason would have stopped me on this fatal incline; sure of myself on every other article, I was lost by this alone. He whom his power puts above men should be above the weaknesses of humanity, without which this excess of strength would only serve to put him in fact below others and below that which the man would have been in himself if he had remained their equal.

All things considered, I believe that I shall do better to throw my magic ring away before it has made me do some foolish thing. If men are determined to see me other than I am, and if my aspect irritates their injustice, to rob them of this sight it is necessary to fly them, but not to conceal myself in their midst: it is for them to conceal themselves before me, to conceal their manœuvres from me, to fly the light of day, to bury themselves in the earth like moles. As for me, let

them see me if they can, so much the better; but that
is impossible to them; they will never see in my place
anything but the Jean-Jacques whom they have made,
and whom they have made according to their desire
to hate at their ease. I should be wrong in being
moved at the way they see me; I ought not to take
away real interest in it, because it is not I whom they
see thus.

The result I deduce from all these reflections is that
I have never been truly accustomed to civil society
where all is worry, obligation, duty, and where my
natural independence renders me always incapable of
the subjections necessary to whoever wishes to live
amongst men. So long as I act freely, I am good and
do nothing but good; but, as soon as I feel the yoke,
whether of necessity, or of men, I become a rebel or
rather, restive: then I am nothing. When it is necessary
to do the contrary of my will, I do not do it, whatever
may chance; I do not even carry out my own will, because I am weak. I abstain from acting, because all my
weakness is in action, all my force is negative, and all
my sins are of omission, rarely of commission. I have
never believed that a man's freedom consisted in
doing what he wished, but rather in not doing
what he did not wish, and this is what I have
always claimed, often preserved, and through which
I have created the most scandal amongst my contemporaries; because, as for them, who are active, stirring,
ambitious, detesting liberty in others and not wishing

it for themselves, provided that they can sometimes work their will, or rather dominate that of another, they waſte all their lives in doing that which is repugnant to them, and do not omit anything base in order to have power. Their wrong has not then been that of chasing me from society like a useless member, but to proscribe me as a pernicious member —because I have done very little good, I admit; but as for evil, it has not entered into my will during life, and I doubt if there is any man in the world who has really done less evil than I.

SEVENTH PROMENADE

THE gathering together of my long reveries has scarcely commenced, and already I feel that it touches its end. Another amusement succeeds to it, absorbs me, and robs me even of the time for dreaming: I yield myself to it with an enthusiasm which is extravagant, and which makes me laugh myself when I think on it; but I do not yield myself less, because, in my present situation, I have no other rule of conduct except to follow my inclination without constraint in everything. I can do nothing with my destiny. I have only innocent inclinations, and all the judgments of men being henceforward nothing for me, wisdom itself demands that in what remains within my grasp I should do all that pleases me either in public, or in private, without any other rule than my fancy, and no other limit than the little strength that remains to me. Here I am then with my hay for nourishment, and my botany for sole occupation. Already old, I acquired the first taste for it in Switzerland, from a doctor of Ivernois, and I botanised happily enough during my wanderings, to gather a passable knowledge of the vegetable kingdom; but having become more than a sexagenarian and sedentary in Paris, the strength for long botanising walks began to fail me, and, moreover being sufficiently devoted to my music-copying not to need another occupation, I had abandoned this amusement which was not necessary to me; I had sold my herbal, I sold my books, content to see again sometimes the common plants which I found about Paris, in my walks. During this interval, the little I knew was almoſt effaced from my memory and much more rapidly than it was fixed there.

All of a sudden, aged over sixty-five, deprived of the little memory I have, and of the ſtrength which remains to me to explore the fields, without a guide, without books, without a garden, without a herbal, I have returned to this folly, but with even more ardour than I had in yielding myself to it for the firſt time: now I am seriously busied with the wise projeƈt of learning by heart all the "Vegetable Kingdom" of Murray, and of underſtanding all the known plants upon earth. Not being able to afford to buy botany books, I have undertaken to copy out those that have been lent me; and, resolved to remake a richer herbal than the firſt, while waiting to put in all the plants of the sea and the Alps, and all the trees of India, I begin cheaply with chickweed, chervil, borage, and rag-wort; I botanise cunningly in the cage of my birds, and at every new blade of grass that I meet, I say with satisfaƈtion: Here is another plant.

I do not seek to juſtify myself in following this

fantasy; I think it very reasonable, persuaded that in my present position, to yield myself to amusements which please me is a great wisdom and a great virtue; it is a way to prevent any leaven of vengeance or of hatred from germinating in my heart; and to discover a taste for some amusement in his lot, a man must certainly be purified of all angry passions. It is avenging myself upon my persecutors in my own way; I could not punish them more cruelly than to be happy despite them.

Yes, without a doubt, reason permits, demands even, that I should yield myself to every inclination which attracts me; and that nothing should prevent me from following it; but it does not teach me why this inclination attracts me nor what attraction I find in a vain study without profit, without progress, and that old, doddering, already bent and heavy, without facility, without memory, it should take me back to the exercises of youth and the lessons of a schoolboy; this is a bizarre fact I should like to understand. It seems to me that if explained it might throw some light upon the knowledge of myself, to the acquisition of which I have devoted my latest leisure.

I have sometimes thought profoundly, but scarcely with pleasure, almost always against my will, and, as it were, by force. Reverie relaxes and amuses me, reflection wearies and saddens me. To think has always been a painful occupation for me and one without charm. Sometimes my reveries end up in meditation, but more often my meditations end up in reverie; and during these wanderings, my soul ſtrays and soars in the universe, upon the wings of the imagination, in ecſtasies which surpass every other enjoyment.

As long as I taſted this in all its purity, every other occupation was always insipid to me; but when once I was thrown into the literary career by outside impulses and felt the fatigue of mental labour and the annoyance of an unfortunate celebrity, I felt at the same time my sweet reveries weaken and become tepid; and soon forced despite myself to occupy myself with my sad situation, I could rarely find these dear ecſtasies which for fifty years have held the place of fortune and of glory for me, with no other expenditure than that of time, and have made me, in idleness, the happieſt of mortals.

I had even to fear, in my reveries, that my imagination, diſturbed by my misfortunes, would turn its aƈtivity in that direƈtion only, and that the continual feeling of my woes, oppressing my heart by degrees, would finally caſt me down with their weight. In this ſtate, an inſtinƈt which is natural to me, making me fly every saddening idea, imposed silence upon my imagination, and, fixing my attention upon those objeƈts which surrounded me, made me, for the firſt time, absorb in detail the speƈtacle of Nature, which I had scarcely contemplated except in mass and in its whole.

REVERIES OF A SOLITARY

The trees, the shrubs, the plants, are the ornamentation and the vestment of the earth. Nothing is so sad as the aspect of a naked and treeless country, which displays to the eye nothing but stones, soil, and sands; but, vivified by Nature, and reclad in its wedding robe, in the midst of watercourses and the song of the birds, the earth offers to man, in the harmony of its three kingdoms, a spectacle full of life, of interest and of charm, the one spectacle in the world of which his eyes and his heart are never weary.

The more a contemplator has a sensitive soul, the more he yields himself to ecstasies which excite in him this harmony. A profound and pleasing reverie then fills his senses, and he loses himself with a delicious intoxication in the immensity of the beautiful system with which he feels himself identified. Then all particular objects escape him; he does not see and does not feel anything but everything. It is necessary that some particular circumstance should gather together his ideas and circumscribe his imagination, in order for him to observe in part this universe which he struggles to embrace.

This naturally happened to me when my heart, oppressed by distress, recalled and concentrated all its movements on itself in order to preserve the remains of fervour which were ready to evaporate and to disappear, in the prostration I gradually experienced. I wandered carelessly through the woods and the mountains, not daring to think, for fear of increasing my griefs. My imagination which refuses itself to painful objects, let my senses yield themselves to the light but sweet impressions of surrounding objects. My eyes wandered ceaselessly from one to the other, and it was not possible that in so great a variety it should not find something to hold them despite themselves, and keep them fixed for a long period.

I acquired a taste for this recreation of the eyes, which in misfortune reposes, amuses, distracts the mind and suspends the feeling of grief. The nature of the objects greatly aids this diversion, and renders it more seductive. Delicate odours, strong colours, the most elegant forms, seem to dispute together for the right to hold one's attention. It is not necessary to love pleasure in order to yield to sensations so sweet; and, if this result does not occur with all those who are smitten by them, it is, in some, a lack of natural sensibility, and in the greater part, because their mind is too much occupied by other ideas and does not yield except stealthily to the objects which strike their senses.

Another thing contributes to remove the attention of people of taste from the vegetable world—that is, the habit of seeking in plants nothing but drugs and remedies. Theophrastus was attracted for a different reason, and this philosopher may be looked upon as the sole botanist of antiquity: he is scarcely known amongst us; but thanks to a certain Dioscorides, a great compiler of recipes, and to his commentators, medicine had taken possession of plants in the form of simples to such an extent that people only see in them what is not there to see—that is to say, the pretended virtues which it pleases three-quarters of mankind to attribute to them. They cannot understand that the vegetable organisation should merit some attention for its own sake; people who pass their lives in learnedly arranging a few shells mock at botany as a useless study when it is not supplemented, as they say, by that of the properties; that is to say, when one does not abandon the observation of Nature, which does not lie and says nothing about all this, in order to yield oneself entirely to the authority of men, who are liars and who affirm many things which must be believed upon their word, founded itself most frequently upon the authority of another. Stop in a flowering plain and examine successively the flowers with which it glows; those who see you doing this, taking you for a quacksalver, will ask for herbs to heal the itch of children, the scabies of men, or the glanders of horses.

This disgusting prejudice is destroyed in part in other countries, and especially in England, thanks to Linnæus, who has taken botany a little away from schools of pharmacy to return it to natural history and to economic use; but in France, where this study has least penetrated among any people of the world, people have remained so barbarous in this respect that a clever man from Paris, seeing in London a connoisseur's garden, full of trees and rare plants, cried out, for all eulogy, " There is a fine garden for an apothecary." According to this view, the first apothecary was Adam, because it is not easy to imagine a garden better furnished with plants than that of Eden.

These medicinal ideas are assuredly not able to render the study of botany agreeable; they spoil the glory of the fields, the glitter of flowers, dry up the freshness of the woods, render the verdure and the shades insipid and disgusting: all these charming and gracious structures interest very little anyone who does wish to bray them in a mortar, and no one will go seeking garlands for shepherdesses among herbs for enemas.

None of this pharmacopœia sullied my rustic pictures; nothing was further from my mind than cordials and plasters. I have often thought, when looking closely upon the fields, the hedgerows, the woods and their numerous inhabitants, that the Vegetable Kingdom was a magazine of food given by Nature to men and beasts; but it never entered my mind to think of seeking drugs or remedies there. I do not see anything in these diverse products, which indicates for me such an usage; and Nature would have shown us the way to choose, if she had prescribed it for us, as she has done for vegetables. I even feel that the pleasure I take in walking about the groves would be poisoned by the sentiment of human infirmities, if it allowed me to think of the fever, the stone, the gout, and epilepsy. For the rest, I do not deny to plants the great virtues which are attributed to them; I only say that in supposing these virtues to be real, it is pure malice in sick men for them to continue to be so; because among all the maladies which men have given themselves, there is not a single one which twenty sorts of herbs do not radically heal.

These tendencies of the mind, which always bring back everything to our material interests, which make us seek for profit or remedies everywhere, and which would make us regard with indifference the whole of Nature if we were always well, have never been mine. I feel myself of a contrary opinion to other men concerning them: all which concerns my needs saddens and spoils my thoughts, and never have I found true charms in the pleasures of the mind save by losing entirely the interest of my body. Thus, even if I myself believed in medicine, and even if its remedies were agreeable, I should never find, in occupying myself with it, those delights which a pure and disinterested contemplation gives, and my soul could not exalt itself and soar above nature, so long as I felt it held in the chains of my body. Moreover, without ever having had any great confidence in medicine, I have had much in doctors whom I esteemed, whom I loved, and to whom I allowed full authority in governing my body. Fifteen years of experience have made me wise at my own expense; I have returned to the law of my nature, and have thereby recovered my first health. If the doctors had no other reason for complaint against me, who would be astonished at their hatred ? I am the living proof of the vanity of their art and the uselessness of their attentions.

No, nothing personal, nothing which concerns the interest of my body, can truly occupy my soul. I do not meditate, do not dream ever more delightfully than when I forget myself. I feel ecstasies, inexpressible ravishments, in mingling myself with the system of beings, so to speak, in identifying myself with the whole of Nature. So long as men were my brothers, I made projects of earthly felicity; these projects being always relative to the whole, I could not be happy except in public felicity, and never has the idea of a particular happiness touched my heart except when I have seen my brothers seeking theirs in my misery. Then, not to hate them, it was necessary to fly them; then, taking refuge in the common mother, I have sought in her arms to withdraw myself from the attacks of her children; I have become solitary, or, as they say, unsociable and misanthropic, because the wildest solitude appears to me preferable to the society of the wicked, which only feeds upon betrayal and hatreds.

Compelled to abstain from thinking, for fear of thinking of my sorrows despite myself: forced to restrain the remains of a strong but languishing imagination, which so much distress might eventually terrify; forced to attempt to forget the men who weigh me down with ignominy and outrage for fear leſt indignation should at laſt embitter me againſt them, I could not concentrate myself entirely in myself, because my expansive soul seeks, despite what I feel, to extend its feelings and its exiſtence over other beings, and I cannot, as once, throw myself head foremoſt into this vaſt ocean of Nature, because my faculties, enfeebled and relaxed, do not find objeċts sufficiently determined and fixed, sufficiently within my grasp, to hold firmly to them, and because I do not feel myself ſtrong enough to swim in the chaos of former ecſtasies. My ideas are scarcely more than sensations, and the sphere of my underſtanding does not surpass the objeċts with which I am immediately surrounded.

Flying from men, seeking solitude, not imagining any more, thinking even less, yet ſtill dowered with a lively temperament, which keeps me far from languishing and melancholy apathy, I began to intereſt myself in all that surrounded me, and by a very natural inſtinċt I gave the preference to the moſt agreeable objeċts. The Mineral Kingdom has nothing in itself either amiable or attraċtive; its riches, enclosed in the breaſt of the earth, seem to have been removed from the gaze of man in order not to tempt his cupidity; they are there like a reserve to serve one day as a supplement to the true wealth which is more within his grasp, and for which he loses taſte according to the extent of his corruption. Then he is compelled to call in industry, to struggle, and to labour to alleviate his miseries; he searches the entrails of earth; he goes seeking to its centre, at the risk of his life and at the expense of his health, for imaginary goods in place of the real good which the earth offers of herself if he knew how to enjoy it. He flies from the sun and the day, which he is no longer worthy to see; he buries himself alive, and does well, not being worthy of living in the light of day. There quarries, pits, forges, furnaces, a battery of anvils, hammers, smoke and fire, succeed to the fair images of his rustic labours. The wan faces of the unhappy people who languish in the poisonous vapours of mines, of black forgemen, of hideous cyclops, are the spectacle which the working of the mine substitutes, in the heart of the earth for that of green fields and flowers, the azure sky, amorous shepherds and robust labourers upon its surface.

It is easy, I admit, to go gathering sand and stone, to fill one's pockets and one's study with it, and to give oneself the airs of a naturalist; but those who attach themselves and limit themselves to these sorts of collections are, ordinarily, ignorant rich people who seek only for the pleasure of display. To profit by the study of minerals, it is necessary to be a chemist and a physicist; it is necessary to make difficult and costly experiments, to work in laboratories, to expend much money and time with charcoal, crucibles, furnaces, retorts, in stifling smoke and vapours, always at the risk of one's life, and often at the expense of one's health. From all this dreary and fatiguing labour comes, ordinarily, much less knowledge than pride: and where is the most mediocre chemist who does not believe that he has penetrated into all the great operations of Nature because he has found, probably by chance, a few little combinations of the art?

The Animal Kingdom is more within our grasp and certainly deserves more to be studied; but finally, has not this study also its difficulties, its embarrassments, its disgusts and its worries, above all for a solitary who has not, either in his play or his labour, any hope of assistance from anyone? How to observe, dissect, study, understand the birds in the air, the fish in the water, the quadrupeds more swift than the wind, more strong than men, and which are not more disposed to come and offer themselves to my researches than I am to run after them in order to make them submit by force? I might have recourse to snails, worms, flies, and I might pass my life in getting out of breath by running after butterflies, and impale poor insects, dissect mice when I could find them, or corpses of beasts when I found them dead. The study of animals is nothing without anatomy; it is by this that one learns to classify and to distinguish the genera, the species. To study them for their behaviour, their characters, it is necessary to have birdcages, vivariums, menageries; it is necessary to constrain them, in whatever manner that can be, to remain assembled near one; I have not the taste, nor the means to retain them in captivity, nor the necessary agility to follow them in their tracks when they are at liberty. I should be compelled then to study them dead, to tear them up, to disarticulate their bones, to grope at leisure in their palpitating entrails! What a frightful equipage is an anatomical amphitheatre!—stinking corpses, dripping and livid flesh, blood, disgusting entrails, frightful skeletons, pestilential vapours! It is not there, upon my word, that Jean Jacques will go seeking his amusements.

Brilliant flowers enamelling the meadows, fresh shade, rivulets, groves, verdure, come and purify my imagination defiled by all these hideous objects. My soul, dead to all vast questions, can no longer be moved except by sensible objects; I have only sensations, and it is through them alone that pain and pleasure can reach me here below. Attracted by the charming objects which surround me, I consider them, I contemplate them, I compare them, I learn finally to classify them, and there I am all of a sudden as much a botanist as any one needs to be who does not wish to study Nature except to find perpetually new reasons for loving her!

I do not seek to instruct myself; it is too late. However, I have never noticed that so much science ever contributed to the happiness of life; but I seek to give myself sweet and simple amusements, which I can enjoy without pain and which distract me from my evils. It costs me nothing, nor need

I take trouble in wandering carelessly from herb to herb, from plant to plant, in order to examine them, to compare their divers characters, to mark their similarities and their differences, in short to observe the vegetable organisation so as to follow the growth and the play of these living machines, to seek with success sometimes their general laws, the reason and the end of their diverse structures, and to yield myself to the charms of a grateful admiration for the Hand which allows me to enjoy all this.

Plants seem to have been sown with profusion upon the earth, like the stars in heaven—to invite men, through the attraction of pleasure and of curiosity, to the study of Nature. But stars are placed far from us; it is necessary to make preliminary studies, to have instruments, machines, very long ladders, to reach them and bring them within our reach. Plants are there naturally; they are born under our feet, and in our hands, so to speak; and if the smallness of their essential parts sometimes removes them from our sight, the instruments which will enable us to see them are much easier to use than those of astronomy. Botany is the study of an idle and unemployed solitary; a needle and a magnifying lens are all the apparatus that is necessary for him to have. He walks about, he wanders freely from one object to another; he makes a review of every flower with interest and curiosity; and as soon as he commences to grasp the laws of their structure, he tastes a pleasure without stain in observing them, as

lively as if it cost him much. There is in this
leisurely occupation a charm which is only felt when
the passions are calmed, but which alone suffices to
render life happy and sweet; but as soon as there is
mingled a motive of interest or of vanity, either to
fill empty places or to make books, as soon as we
only wish to learn in order to teach, and only
gather specimens to become an author or professor,
all this sweet charm evaporates, we see in the plants
nothing but the instruments of our passions, we
do not find any true pleasure in their study, we
do not wish to know but to show that we know,
and in the woods we are only in the theatre of
the world, occupied with the care of getting ourselves admired; or rather, limiting ourselves to the
botany of the study and the garden at the most,
instead of observing plants in Nature, we only
occupy ourselves with systems and methods; an
eternal matter for dispute, which does not make one
plant the better known, and does not throw any true
light upon natural history or the Vegetable Kingdom
—hence these hatreds, these jealousies, which the
competition for celebrity excites among botanical
authors, as much and more than among other scholars.
Distorting this amiable study, they transplant it into
the midst of cities and academies, where it degenerates
no less than the exotic plants in the gardens of the
curious.

Very different opinions have made for me of this

study a sort of passion which fills the void of all those which I have no longer. I mount the rocks, the mountains, I bury myself in the valleys, in the woods, to conceal myself, as far as is possible, from the remembrance of men and the approaches of evilly-disposed people. It seems to me that under the shade of the woods I am forgotten, free, and peaceful, as if I had no more enemies, or as if the foliage of the woods would guard me from their approaches as it withdraws them from my memory; and I imagine in my stupidity that, when I am not thinking of them, they do not think of me. I find so great a sweetness in this illusion, that I should yield myself entirely to it, if my situation, my weakness, and my needs would permit. The more the solitude in which I live is profound, the more I require some object to fill the void; and those which my imagination refuses or my memory rejects are supplemented by the spontaneous productions that the earth, not forced by men, offers to my eyes on all sides. The pleasure of going into a solitude to seek for new plants overlaps that of escaping from my persecutors; and having arrived in places where I do not see any trace of men, I breathe more at my ease, as in a retreat where their hatred does not pursue me.

I shall remember all my life a botanical excursion I made one day in the direction of the Robaila, a mountain belonging to Chief Justice Clerc. I was alone, I plunged into the ravines of the mountain; and from wood to wood, from rock to rock, I attained a spot so hidden that I have never seen a wilder scene in my life. Black pines mingled with prodigious beeches, several of which had fallen from old age and interlaced themselves with each other, closed this retreat with impenetrable barriers; such intervals as were left in this sombre enclosure did not show beyond anything but rocks broken into peaks, and horrible precipices, which I dared not look at except by lying down flat on my ſtomach. The eagle owl, the small owl and the buzzard made their cries heard in the chasms of the mountain; some small birds, rare but familiar, tempered, however, the horror of this solitude; there I found the toothed *Heptaphyllos*, the *Cyclamen*, the *Nidus avis*, the large *Lacerpitium*, and some other plants which charmed and amused me for a long time; but insensibly dominated by the ſtrong impression of objeƈts, I forgot botany and plants, I seated myself upon cushions of *Lycopodium* and moss, and allowed myself to dream at ease, thinking that I was there in a refuge unknown to all the universe, and where persecutors would not unearth me. A sentiment of pride mingled soon with this reverie. I compared myself to those great travellers who discover a deserted island, and I said to myself with complaisance: "Without a doubt I am the firſt mortal who has penetrated here." I looked on myself almoſt as another Columbus. While I prided myself on this idea, I heard not far off from me a certain clicking sound which I thought I recognised;

I listened; the same sound repeated itself, and was multiplied. Surprised and curious, I got up, and pierced through a mass of undergrowth on the side from which the sound came, and in a coomb, at twenty paces from the place where I believed I was the first to come, I found a stocking-factory !

I cannot express the confused and contradictory agitation which I felt in my heart at this discovery. My first sensation was a feeling of joy at finding myself amongst human beings when I had believed myself to be totally alone; but this sensation, more rapid than the lightning flash, soon gave place to a painful feeling, more lasting, as if not even in the caves of Alps had I been able to escape from the cruel hands of men determined to torment me. For I felt quite sure that there were perhaps not two men in this factory who were not initiated into the plot which the preacher Montmollin had headed against me, and which drew from further off its first motives. I hastened to cast off this sad notion, and I ended by laughing at myself, and at my puerile vanity, and at the comic manner in which I had been punished.

But, in fact, who ever could have expected to find a factory under a precipice! It is only in Switzerland that one finds this mixture of savage nature and human industry. The whole of Switzerland is nothing, so to speak, but a great city whose roads, longer and wider than those of the Faubourg Saint-Antoine, are sown with forests, cut by mountains and whose houses, scattered and isolated, do not communicate with each other except through English gardens. I recall on this subject another botanising trip which Du Peyron, d'Escherny, Colonel de Pury, Justice Clerc, and myself had made some time before on the mountain of Chasseron, from the summit of which one can see seven lakes. We were told that there was only a single house on this mountain, and we should surely not have guessed the profession of the man who inhabited it, if it had not been added that he was a bookseller, and one who carried on his business successfully in this country. It seems to me that a single fact of that sort makes Switzerland better known than all the descriptions of travellers.

Here is another of the same kind, or almost so, which is equally characteristic of a very different people. During my sojourn at Grenoble I often made small botanical excursions outside the town with the Sieur Bouvier, a lawyer of that country; not that he knew or loved botany, but because having made himself my body-guard, he made it a law, as much as possible, not to quit my side so much as a step. One day we were walking along the Isère in a place full of thorn-poplars. I saw on these shrubs ripe fruits; I had the curiosity to taste them, and finding in them a slight acidity very agreeable, I began to eat these berries to refresh myself: the Sieur Bouvier remained at my side without imitating me, and said nothing. One of his friends came up, who, seeing me nibble at these berries, said: "Sir, what are you doing there? Don't you know that fruit is poisonous?"—"Poison!" said I, greatly surprised.—"Without a doubt," he replied; "and everyone knows it so well that no one in the country attempts to taste it." I looked at the Sieur Bouvier, and said: "Why did you not tell me?"—"Ah, sir," he replied, in a tone of respect, "I did not dare take such a liberty." I started to laugh at this provincial humility, while discontinuing nevertheless my little feast. I was persuaded, as I am still, that every natural production, agreeable to taste, cannot be harmful to the body, or at least is not so except by its excess. However, I admit that I paid some attention to myself for the rest of the day; but I got off with nothing worse than a little disquiet; I supped very well, slept better, and awakened in the morning in perfect health, after having swallowed the day before fifteen or twenty berries of that terrible *Hippophæ*, which poisons with the smallest dose, according to what everyone told me in Grenoble the next day. This adventure seemed to me so amusing that I never recall it without laughing at the singular discretion of the advocate Bouvier.

All my botany excursions, the different impressions of the locality of objects which have struck me, the ideas which they have called up in me, the incidents which are mixed up with them—all this has left me impressions which are renewed by the aspect of plants gathered in the same places. I shall never see again those

154

beautiful landscapes, rocks, forests, groves, mountains, the aspect of which has always touched my heart; but now that I can no more traverse those pleasant lands, I have only to open my herbal, and soon I am transported there. The fragments of plants which I have collected there suffice to recall to me all that magnificent spectacle. This herbal is for me a journal of botanical excursions, which has made me recommence them with a new delight, and has produced the effect of the vision which formerly painted them to my eyes.

It is the chain of accessory ideas which has attached me to botany. It reassembles and recalls to my imagination all the ideas which formerly gave it pleasure; the meadows, the waters, the woods, solitude, peace above all, and the rest one finds in the midst of all this, are retraced by it incessantly upon my memory. It makes me forget the persecutions of men, their hatred, their scorn, their outrages, and all the evils with which they have repaid my tender and sympathetic attachment for them. It transports me into peaceful habitations, in the midst of simple good people, such as those with whom I once lived. It recalls to me both my youth and my innocent pleasures; it makes me enjoy them over again, and often renders me happy still, in the midst of the saddest lot that has ever befallen a human being.

EIGHTH PROMENADE

IN meditating upon the tendencies of my soul in all the situations of my life, I have been extremely struck to see so little proportion between the diverse combinations of my destiny and the habitual feelings of well or evil being with which they have affected me. The diverse intervals of my short prosperities have allowed me scarcely any agreeable recollection of the intimate and permanent manner in which they have affected me; and, on the other hand, in all the miseries of my life, I have felt myself constantly filled with tender feelings, touching and delicious, which, pouring a salutary balm upon the wounds of my broken heart, seem to convert the pain into pleasure, the charming remembrance of which alone comes back to me, free from the evils which I felt at the same time. It seems to me that I have tasted more sweetness of living, that I really lived more, when my feelings were compressed, so to speak, about my heart by destiny, and did not allow themselves to evaporate on all the exterior objects which men esteem and which form the sole occupation of those people who are believed to be happy.

When everything was in order about me, when I was content with all that surrounded me, and with the sphere in which I had to live, I filled it with my affection.

EIGHTH PROMENADE

My expansive soul stretched out towards other objects;
and, always drawn far from myself by tastes of a thousand kinds, by pleasing attachments which incessantly
occupied my heart, I forgot myself to some extent; I
was entirely devoted to that which was strange to me,
and experienced in the continual agitation of my heart
all the vicissitude of human things.   This stormy life
did not leave me either peace within or rest outside.
Happy in appearance, I had not a sentiment which
could endure the test of reflection, and with which
I could truly please myself.   Never was I perfectly
content either with the world or myself.   The tumult
of the world deafened me, and solitude wearied me; I
felt the need to change places unceasingly, and I was
not happy anywhere.   I was fêted however, well wished,
well received, caressed everywhere; I had not an enemy,
not an ill-wisher, not an envious person; as no one
sought but to oblige me, I often had the pleasure myself
of obliging many people, and without wealth, without employment, without supporters, without great
talents well known or well developed, I enjoyed the
advantages attached to all this, and I did not see anyone
in any state whose lot appeared preferable to mine.
What was lacking, then, in order to be happy ?   I do
not know; but I know that I was not happy.   What
is lacking to me to-day to be the most unfortunate
of mortals ?   Nothing that men could do on their
part to make me so.   Yet, in this deplorable state,
I would not change my existence and my destiny

with the most fortunate of them; and I still prefer to be myself in all my misery than to be any of these people in all their prosperity. Reduced to myself alone, I feed myself, it is true, on my own substance, but it is not exhausted. I suffice myself, although I chew a non-existent cud, so to speak, and though my wrecked imagination and my extinguished ideas do not furnish any food to my heart. My soul, offended, weighed down by my organs, weakens from day to day; and under the weight of these heavy masses lacks vigour to leap out from its old envelope, as in the past.

Adversity forces us to recoil upon ourselves; and perhaps it is that which renders it most unendurable to the greater part of men. For myself, who find only faults to reproach myself with, I accuse my weakness, and I console myself; for never has premeditated evil approached my heart.

However, unless I am stupid, how can I contemplate my situation for a moment, without seeing it as horrible as others have made it, and without perishing of sorrow or despair? Far from this, I, the most sensitive of beings, contemplate it and am unmoved; and without a struggle, without making an effort, I see myself almost with indifference in a state, the sight of which no other man perhaps could endure without horror.

How have I come to this? For I was far from this peaceful state of mind at the first suspicion of the plot in which I had long been entangled without having the least perception of it. This new discovery completely upset me. Infamy and treason took me by surprise. What honeſt soul is prepared for this sort of suffering? It would be necessary to merit them in order to fore-see them. I fell into all the snares which were digged beneath my feet. Indignation, fury, delirium seized upon me; I loſt my direction. My head was turned, and in the horrible darkness in which men have not ceased to keep me plunged, I perceived neither a gleam to guide me, nor a support, nor a foothold to ſtand firmly on and to resiſt the despair which carried me away.

How could I live happy and tranquil in this frightful ſtate? Yet I am ſtill in it and more deeply entangled than ever, and I have rediscovered calm and peace there, and live there happy and tranquil, and I laugh at the unbelievable pains which my persecutors con-tinually give themselves, while I remain in peace, occupied with flowers, with ſtamens and childish things, and I do not even dream of them.

How has this change taken place? Naturally, insensibly, and without pain. The firſt surprise was frightful. I, who felt myself worthy of eſteem and love, I who believed myself honoured, cherished, as I deserved to be, I saw myself suddenly traveſtied into a frightful monſter, such as never exiſted. I saw a whole generation throw themselves entirely into this ſtrange delusion, without any explanation, without doubt, without shame, and without my being able to learn even the cause of this strange revolution. I struggled violently and I only succeeded in entangling myself worse. I tried to force my persecutors to explain themselves; they paid no attention. After tormenting myself for a long time without success, I was forced to take breath. However, I still hoped; I said: a blindness so stupid, a prejudice so absurd, cannot reach the whole of the human race. There are men of sense who do not partake of this delirium; there are just men who detest baseness and treachery. Let me seek, I shall perhaps find a man at last; if I find him, they will be confounded. I have sought in vain; I have not found him. The league against me is universal, without exception, without change; and I am certain of ending my days in this frightful proscription, without ever penetrating its mystery.

In this deplorable state, after long agonies, instead of the despair which seemingly should be finally my lot, I have rediscovered serenity, tranquillity, peace, even happiness, because each day of my life recalls to me with pleasure that of the day before, and that I do not desire a different one for the morrow.

Whence comes this difference? From a single thing: it is that I have learned how to bear the yoke of necessity without murmuring; it is that I was yet struggling to hold on to a thousand things, and that all these holds having successively escaped me, I was reduced to myself alone and finally regained my balance. Pressed on all sides, I remain in equilibrium, because I depend upon no one but myself.

When I set myself with so much ardour against opinion, I still carried its yoke without perceiving it. A man wishes to be esteemed by people whom he esteems; and so long as I could judge men favourably, or at least some men, the judgments they made upon me could not be indifferent to me; I saw that often the judgments of the public are fair; but I did not see that this fairness itself was the result of chance; that the rules upon which men form their opinions are only drawn from their passions or their prejudices, which are derived from them; and that even when they judge well, yet these right judgments are often born from a bad principle, as when they feign to honour in the merit of a man some successes, not from a spirit of justice, but to give themselves an impartial air while calumniating at their ease the same man on other points.

But when, after such long and vain searchings, I saw everything remain without exception in the most iniquitous and absurd system that the infernal spirit could invent; when I saw that, in regard to me, reason was banished from all hands and equity from all hearts; when I saw a frantic generation yield itself entirely to the blind fury of its guides against an unfortunate man who did not do, nor wish, nor return evil to anyone; when, after having vainly sought for a man, it was necessary finally to extinguish my lantern and to cry, " There are no more," then I began to see myself alone on earth and

I understood that my contemporaries were nothing in relation to me but mechanical beings, who only acted upon impulse, and whose actions I could only calculate from the laws of movement: whatever intention, whatever passion I might have supposed in their souls, these would never have explained their conduct towards me in a way that I could understand. Thus, their interior motives ceased to be anything to me; I saw nothing in them except masses differently moved, deprived of all morality in regard to me.

In all the evils which come upon us, we look more to the intention than to the effect; a tile falling from a roof may wound us more seriously, but does not distress us so much as a stone thrown by design from an ill-wishing hand; the blow sometimes falls short, but the intention does not ever miss its object. Material sorrow is that which one feels the least in the attacks which fortune directs against us; and when the unfortunate do not know to whom to ascribe their evils they attribute them to destiny, which they personify, and to which they ascribe eyes and the intelligence to torment them purposely: it is thus that a gambler, irritated by his losses, lashes himself into fury without knowing against whom; he imagines a fate which is turned against him by design to torment him, and finding food for his anger, he arouses and inflames himself against the enemy he has created. The wise man who sees in all the evils that happen to him only the blows of blind necessity does not feel these insensate agitations; he cries out in his sorrow, but without being carried away, without anger; of the evil to which he is the prey he does not feel more than the material side, and the blows which he receives may wound his person, but not one can reach his heart.

It is much to have arrived at this point, but it is not all if we have stopped there; it is indeed to have cut off the evil, but to have left the root; for this root is not in beings who are strange to us, it is in ourselves, and it is there that we must labour to uproot it entirely. That is what I felt perfectly as soon as I began to recover myself; since my reason did not show me anything but absurdities in all the explanations which I tried to find for what had happened to me, I perceived that, since the causes, the instruments, the means of all this were unknown and unexplainable to me, they should be nothing to me; that I should look upon all the details of my destiny as so many acts of pure fatality, in which I should suppose neither direction, nor intention, nor moral cause; that it was necessary to submit myself to fatality without reasoning and without revolt, because that was useless; that, since all I had to do still upon earth was to regard myself as a purely passive creature, I should not use to vain resistance against destiny the strength which remained to me to endure it. That is what I said to myself; my reason, my heart acquiesced, and nevertheless I felt my heart still murmur against it.

Whence came this murmur? I sought, I found it; it came from my self-love, which after feeling indignation against mankind, raised itself up against reason.

This discovery was not so easy to make as one might believe, because a persecuted and innocent man for a long time mistakes the pride of his small individuality for a pure love of justice, but the true source, once well known, is easy to quench, or at least to divert. Self-esteem is the greatest motive force of proud souls; self-love, fertile in illusions, disguises itself and is mistaken for this esteem; but when the deceit is finally discovered, and self-love cannot conceal itself any more, thenceforward there is nothing more to fear, and though a man stifles it with difficulty, he at least subjugates it easily.

I never had much tendency to self-love; but this factitious passion was exalted in me by society, and above all when I was an author; even then I had perhaps less of it than another, but I had it prodigiously. The terrible lessons I have received soon put it back into its first bounds: it began by revolting against injustice, but ended by disdaining it; by falling back upon my soul, by cutting the external relations which render it exacting, by renouncing comparisons and preferences, it is content that I should suffice myself. Thus, becoming again love of myself, it has returned to the order of nature, and has delivered me from the yoke of opinion.

From that time on I have rediscovered peace and

almost felicity in my soul; for, in whatever situation a man finds himself, it is only through himself that he is constantly unhappy. When self-love is silent and reason speaks, it consoles us finally for all the ills that it was not in our power to avoid; it destroys them the more readily when they do not act immediately upon us; because we are sure then to avoid their most poignant attacks by ceasing to occupy ourselves with them. They are nothing for him who does not think of them; offences, vengeances, wrongs, outrages, injustices, are nothing for him who saw in the evils he endures only the evil itself and not the intention, for him whose place in his own esteem does not depend on what it pleases others to grant him. In whatever fashion men wish to see me, they cannot change my being; and despite their power, and despite all their cunning intrigues, I shall continue, whatever they do, to be what I am despite them. It is true that their intentions towards me influence my real situation; the barrier which they have put between themselves and myself robs me of every resource of subsistence and of assistance in my old age and need. It makes even money useless to me, because it cannot procure me the services which are necessary to me; there is no commerce, no reciprocal bargain, no correspondence between them and myself. Alone in the midst of them, my sole resource is myself, and at my age and in my present state that resource is feeble. These are great ills; but they have

lost all their power over me since I have learned to
endure them without irritation. Those places where
real necessity is felt are always rare; foresight and
imagination multiply them, and this continuity of
feelings makes us uneasy and unhappy. For my part,
though I may well know that to-morrow I shall suffer,
I am calm if I do not suffer to-day; I am not affected
by the ills I foresee, but only by those I now feel, and
they are reduced to very little. Alone, ill, and abandoned in my bed, I could die of indigence, of cold
and hunger, without anyone being afflicted. But
what matter if I am not afflicted myself, and if I am
affected as little as others by my fate, whatever it may
be? Is it nothing, above all at my age, to have
learned to look at life and death, illness and health,
riches and misery, glory and defamation, with the
same indifference? All other old men are disquieted
about everything, I am disquieted at nothing; whatever may happen, all is indifferent to me; and this indifference is not the work of my wisdom but of my
enemies, and becomes a compensation for the evils
which they do to me. By rendering me insensible
to adversity, they have done me more good than if
they had spared me its attacks; in not experiencing
it, I might always fear it, instead of which, by subju-
gating it, I do not fear it at all.

This disposition leaves me in the midst of the changes
of my life, to the negligence of my nature, almost as fully
as if I were living in the most complete prosperity; out-

side the short moments in which I am recalled, by the presence of objeets, to the moft dolourous inquietudes, all the reft of the time, delivered by my inclinations to the affeetions which attraet me, my heart is nourished ftill by the sentiments for which it was born, and I play with imaginary beings who produce them and share them, as if these beings really exifted; they exift for me who have created them, and I do not fear either that they may betray me, or that they may abandon me; they will laft as long as my griefs themselves, and will suffice to make me forget them.

Everything brings me back to the happy and sweet life for which I was born; I pass three-quarters of my life, either occupied with inftruetive and even agreeable objeets to which I yield my spirit and my senses with delight, or with the children of my fantasy that I create according to my heart, inter- course with whom nourishes its feelings, or with myself alone, content with myself, and already full of the happiness that I feel is owing to me. In all this the love of myself does everything, and self-con- ceit does not enter into it. It is not so with the sad moments that I pass ftill in the midft of men, the plaything of their traitorous caresses, of their swollen and derisory compliments, of their honey-sweet ma- lignity: in whatever fashion that I may then behave, self-conceit plays its part. The hatred and the ani- mosity that I see in their hearts, through this coarse envelope, rend my own heart with sorrow; and the idea of being so foolishly taken for a dupe adds to this grief a puerile annoyance, fruit of a foolish self-conceit of which I feel all the stupidity, but which I cannot subjugate. The efforts which I have made to harden myself to these insulting and mocking looks are unbelievable: a hundred times have I passed on the public promenade and in the most frequented spots with the sole aim of exercising myself in these cruel struggles; not only I have not been able to succeed, but I have not even advanced at all, and all my painful but vain efforts have left me as easy to trouble, to distress and to arouse to indignation as beforehand.

Dominated by my senses, whatever I may do, I have never been able to resist their impressions, and as long as the object acts upon them, my heart does not cease to be affected; but these passing affections do not last any longer than the sensation which causes them. The presence of the hateful man affects me violently; but as soon as he disappears, the impression ceases: at the instant that I do not see him any more, I do not think of him any more. I may know well that he will occupy himself with me, I shall not occupy myself with him; the evil which I do not feel immediately does not affect me in any way; the persecutor whom I do not see is nothing to me. I feel the advantage which this position gives to those who control my destiny. Let them control it then at their ease; I much prefer that they should torment me, without resistance, than that I shall be forced to think of them to shield myself from their blows.

This action of my senses on my heart is the one torment of my life. In the places where I do not see anyone, I do not think of my destiny any more, I do not feel it, I do not suffer; I am happy and content without diversion, without an obstacle. But I rarely escape from some sensible injury; and when I think of it the least, a gesture, a sinister look, which I perceive, an envenomed word which I hear, an evil-wisher whom I encounter, suffice to upset me; all that I can do in such a case is to forget speedily and to take flight; the trouble of my heart disappears with the object which causes it, and I return to calm as soon as I am alone; or if anything disquiets me, it is the fear of finding in my way some new cause for pain. That is my sole grief; but it suffices to spoil my happiness. I lodge in the midst of Paris; on going out, I sigh for the country and solitude; but it is necessary to seek it so far that before I can breathe at my ease I find in my road a thousand objects which contract my heart, and the half of my day passes in agonies before I have attained the refuge that I seek. Happy at least when I am allowed to continue on my way! The moment when I escape the crowd of evil-doers is delightful, and as soon as I see myself under the trees, in the midst of verdure, I believe that I am in the terrestrial paradise, and I taste an inner pleasure as lively as if I were the happiest of mortals.

I remember perfectly that, during my short period of prosperity, these same solitary walks, which are to-day so delicious, were insipid and tiresome to me; when I was with someone in the country, the need of exercising myself and breathing the fresh air made me often go out alone, and, escaping like a thief, I went to walk in the park or in the country; but far from finding the happy calm which I find to-day, I carried with me the agitation of vain ideas which had occupied me in the salon; the remembrance of the company which I had left there followed me. In solitude, the fog of self-conceit and the tumult of the world darkened to my eyes the freshness of the groves and troubled the peace of my retreat: however much I might fly to the depths of the woods, an importunate crowd followed me everywhere, and veiled all Nature for me. It is only after having detached myself from social passions and from their dismal throng that I have refound Nature with all its charms.

Convinced of the impossibility of repressing these first involuntary movements, I have ceased all my efforts: at every blow I have allowed my blood to kindle, choler and indignation to seize upon my senses; I yield to nature this first explosion which all my strength cannot stop nor suspend. I seek only to stop the sequel before its effect has been produced. Glittering eyes, a blushing face, the trembling of limbs, suffocating palpitations, all this belongs to the body only, and reasoning can do nothing with it. But after

having left to nature its first outburst, one can become
one's own master by resuming little by little one's
senses; it is that which I have attempted to do for a
long time without success, but finally more happily;
and, ceasing to employ my strength in vain resistance,
I await the moment of conquest by letting my reason
act, because it does not ever speak to me except when
it can make itself heard. But what am I saying,
alas, my reason? I should be very wrong to give it
the honour of this triumph, because it has scarcely any
part in it; all comes equally from a versatile temperament which an impetuous wind agitates, but which
returns to calm the instant that the wind ceases to blow;
it is my natural indolence which quiets me. I yield
to all my present impulses: every shock gives me a
strong but brief movement; as soon as there is no
shock the movement ceases, nothing which is com-
municated can prolong itself in me. All the events of
fortune, all the machinations of men, have little grip
upon a man so constituted; to affect me with lasting
sorrows, the impression would have to be renewed at
every moment; because the intervals, however short
they may be, suffice to bring me back to myself.
I know that which pleases men, so long as they can
act upon my senses; but, at the first moment of
relaxation, I become again that which my nature
has determined: whatever they may do, that is my
most constant state, and it is through this, in spite of
destiny, that I taste a happiness for which I feel myself

conftituted.　I have described this ftate in one of my reveries.　It suits me so well, that I do not desire anything else than that it should continue, and I only fear lest it should be troubled.　The evil that men have done me does not touch me in any way: the fear alone of that which they are able to do me is capable of agitating me; but, certain that they have not a new hold by which they can affe&t me with a pleasant sentiment, I laugh at all their plots, and I enjoy myself in spite of them.

NINTH PROMENADE

HAPPINESS is a permanent state which does not seem to be made for men here below; everything upon earth is in a continual flux which does not permit anything to take on a fixed form. Everything changes about us, we change ourselves, and no one can be certain that he will love to-morrow what he loves to-day; thus all our plans of felicity for this life are illusions. Let us profit by contentment of spirit when it comes, let us guard ourselves from driving it away by our fault; but do not let us make plans to enchain it, because these plans are pure follies; I have seen few happy men, perhaps none; but I have often seen contented hearts, and of all the objects which have struck me, it is this that has contented me most myself. I believe that this is a natural result of the power of sensations upon my inner sentiments. Happiness has no external signs; in order to know it, it is necessary to read in the heart of the happy man, but contentment can be read in the eyes, in the carriage, in the accent, in the gait, and seems to communicate itself to whoever perceives it. Is there an enjoyment more sweet than to see an entire people give themselves up to joy on a festival day, and to see all hearts expand to the rays of pleasure which pass rapidly but strongly, through the clouds of life ? . . .

Three days have passed since M. P—— came with extraordinary eagerness to show me the eulogy of Madame Geoffrin by M. d'Alembert. The reading was preceded by long and loud bursts of laughter upon the ridiculous slang of this piece and upon the absurd plays upon words with which he said it was filled : he began to read it laughing heartily. I listened with a serious air which calmed him, and seeing that I did not imitate him, he ceased finally to laugh. The longest and most laboured article of this piece was upon the pleasure which Madame Geoffrin took in seeing children and making them talk; the author drew with reason, from this disposition, a proof of her good-nature; but he did not stop there, and he decidedly accused those who had not the same taste of bad natural disposition and evil thinking, to the point of saying that if those who were being led to the gibbet or the wheel were asked, all would admit that they had not loved children. These assertions made a singular effect in the place where they occurred. Supposing all this to be true, was it the occasion for saying it ? and was it necessary to soil the eulogy of an estimable woman by images of hangings and evil-doers ? I understood easily the motive of this villainous affectation; and when M. P—— had finished reading it, while pointing out what appeared to me good in this eulogy, I added that the author, in writing it, had less love than hatred in his heart.

The next day, the weather being sufficiently fair, although cold, I went to take a walk as far as the Military School, hoping to find there mosses in full flower. While walking, I meditated on the visit of the day before, and upon M. d'Alembert's composition, in which I thought the episodic arrangement had not been made without design; and the mere affectation of bringing this pamphlet to me, from whom they ordinarily conceal everything, showed me sufficiently what was the object. I had put my children in the Foundling Hospital: that was enough to travesty me as an unnatural father, and from there, by extending and caressing this idea, they had little by little drawn the evident consequence that I hated my children; in following by thought the chain of these gradations, I admired with what art human industry can change things from white to black; because I do not believe that any man has loved better than myself to see little children romp and play together; and, often in the street and in promenades, I have stopped to look at their antics and their little games with an interest which I do not observe to be shared by anyone else. The same day when M. P—— came, an hour before his visit, I had a visit from the two little children of Soussoi, the youngest children of my host, the elder of whom was seven; they had come to embrace me so sincerely, and I had returned their caresses so tenderly, that despite the

175

disparity of ages, they had appeared really to enjoy themselves with me, and for myself, I was transported with joy to see that my old face had not rebuffed them; the younger even seemed to come to me so gladly that, more childish than they, I felt myself to be attached to him already by preference, and I saw him leave with as much regret as if he had belonged to me.

I understand that the reproach of having put my children in the Foundling Hospital has easily degenerated, with a little twisting, into that of being an unnatural father and of hating children: however, it is certain that it was the fear of a fate a thousand times worse for them, and almost inevitable through every other way, which determined me the most in this step. More indifferent upon what they might become, and incapable of bringing them up myself, it would have been necessary, in my situation, to have let them be brought up by their mother, who would have spoilt them, and by her family, who would have made monsters of them. I shudder even to think of it; that which Mahomet made of Zeid[1] is nothing in comparison to what would have been done with them in respect to me, and the snares which were held forth to me on this matter in the sequel assure me sufficiently that the plan had been formed. In truth, I was far from foreseeing these atrocious plots: but I knew that the least perilous education for them was

[1] Zeid was Mahomet's adopted son, a Christian. The Prophet fell in love with his wife, and ordered him to divorce her for his benefit.

that of the Foundling Hospital, and I put them there. I would do it again, and with much less doubt if the thing were to do; and I know well that no father is more tender than I should have been for them, if only habit might have aided nature.

If I have made some progress in knowledge of the human heart, it is the pleasure I take in seeing and observing children that has given me this knowledge. This same pleasure, in my youth, was a sort of obstacle to it, for I play with children so gladly and with such a good heart, that I scarcely dream of studying them. But when, as I grew old, I saw that my crooked figure disquieted them I abstained from my importunity: I preferred rather to deprive myself of a pleasure than to trouble their enjoyment; and content then to satisfy myself by watching all their games and their little tricks, I found the reward for my sacrifice in the information which these observations have made me acquire upon the first and true movements of nature, of which all our wise men know nothing. I have consigned to my writings the proof that I was occupied with this research too carefully not to have made it with pleasure; and it would be assuredly the most unbelievable thing in the world, if "Héloïse" and "Émile," were the works of a man who did not love children.

I never had presence of mind, nor the facility of speaking; but since my misfortunes, my tongue and my head are more and more embarrassed; the idea and the proper word escape me equally, and nothing requires a better discernment and a more just choice of expression than the words which we address to children. That which increases in me this embarrassment is the attention of those listening, the interpretations and the weight which they give to all that which comes from a man who, having written expressly for children, is supposed not to have a right to speak to them, except by oracles; this extreme care, and the inaptitude which I feel trouble and disconcert me, and I should be more at my ease before a monarch of Asia than before a child whom I must make babble.

Another inconvenience holds me at present more removed from them, and since my misfortunes I see them always with the same pleasure, but I have not the same familiarity with them. Children do not like old age; the aspect of nature giving way is hideous in their eyes; their repugnance (which I perceive) is heartbreaking, and I prefer to stop caressing them rather than to cause them uneasiness or disgust. This motive, which only affects truly loving souls, is nothing to all our doctors and doctoresses. Madame Geoffrin cared very little whether children took pleasure with her, provided that she had pleasure with them; but for me, this pleasure is worse than nothing; it is negative when it is not shared; and I am no longer in the situation or at the age when I saw the little heart of a child expanding with mine. If this could happen to me ſtill, this pleasure, become more rare, would be but the more lively for me; I felt it, the other morning, by the pleasure I took in caressing the little ones of Soussoi, not only because the nurse who accompanied them did not intimidate me much, and I felt less the need to reſtrain myself before her, but also because the happy air with which they approached me did not quit them, and they did not appear either to be displeased or to be bored with me.

Oh! If I had ſtill some moments of the pure caresses which come from the heart, were it only from a child ſtill in swaddling-clothes; if I could see ſtill in some eyes the joy and contentment of being with me, for how many woes and griefs would not these short but sweet outpourings of my heart repay me! Ah! I should not be obliged to seek among the animals the look of benevolence, which is henceforth refused me among humans. I can judge of them from very few examples, but these are always dear to my memory: here is one which in any other ſtate I should have almoſt forgotten, and whose impression upon me discovers all my misery.

Two years have passed since, going for a walk in the direction of New France, I went on farther: then drawing to the right and wishing to circle round Montmartre, I traversed the village of Clignancourt; I walked diſtraƈted and dreaming without looking about me, when suddenly I felt my knees seized. I looked, and I saw a small child of five or six who pressed my knees with all his strength, looked at me with an air so familiar and so caressing that my entrails were moved; I said to myself: It is thus that I would have treated my own. I took the child in my arms, I kissed it several times in a sort of transport, and then I continued my road. I felt in walking on that something was lacking to me; an awakening need turned me back upon my steps; I reproached myself for having quitted this child so brusquely, I believed I saw in its action, without apparent cause, a sort of inspiration which I ought not to disdain. Finally, yielding to temptation, I returned upon my steps, I ran to the child, I embraced it again and I gave it some money to buy small cakes, the vendor of which was passing by hazard, and I began to make it chatter. I asked who was his father: he showed him to me; he was a cooper of barrels. I was ready to quit the child to go and speak to him, when I saw that I had been forestalled by a man of an evil look, who appeared to me to be one of these spies who follow my track incessantly; while this man spoke into his ear, I saw the looks of the cooper fix themselves attentively upon me, with an air which had nothing friendly about it. This sight gripped my heart upon the instant, and I quitted the father and the child with more promptitude than I had put in returning upon my steps, but with a less agreeable trouble which changed all my feelings. I have often felt them renewed since then; I have passed by Clignancourt many times, in the hope of seeing the child again; but I have seen neither him nor his father, and there has remained of this meeting nothing but a lively remembrance, mixed with sweetness and sadness, like all the emotions which yet penetrate sometimes to my heart.

There is compensation for everything: if my pleasures are rare and brief, I taſte them more acutely when they come, than if they were more familiar; I chew them over, so to speak, by frequent remembrance; and, however rare they may be, if they were pure and without mixture, I should be more happy perhaps than in any prosperity. In extreme misery one finds oneself rich with a little; a beggar who finds a crown is more delighted than a rich man finding a purse of gold. You would laugh if you could see in my soul the impression made by the slighteſt pleasures of this species, which I have been able to snatch from the vigilance of my persecutors: one of the sweeteſt presented itself four or five years ago, and I never recall it without feeling myself ravished with delight at having so well profited by it.

One Sunday we had gone, my wife and I, to dine at the Porte Maillot: after dinner we traversed the Bois de Boulogne, up to the Muette; there we sat down on the grass, in the shade, while waiting for the sun to set, in order to return again slowly through Passy. A score of young girls, conduɑed by a sort of nun, came, some to sit down, the others to play near us. During their play, there came by a wafer-seller, with his drum and his wheel, looking for trade; I saw that the little girls desired wafers very much, and two or three of them who apparently possessed some pennies asked permission to gamble. While the governess hestitated and disputed, I called the wafer-maker and said: Let these young ladies draw out each in turn, and I will pay for all. The word spread throughout the troop a joy which alone would have paid for the expenditure of the whole of my purse, if I had employed it entirely for that.

As I saw that they pressed forward in some confusion, with the consent of the governess I arranged them all on one side, and then passed them to the other side, one after the other, as each had drawn. In order that there should be no white ticket, and that there should come at least one wafer to each of those who won nothing, so that none of them would be absolutely discontented, and to make the party gayer I told the wafer-seller to use his ordinary skill in the contrary sense, by making as many good numbers fall as he could, and that I would account to him. By means of this arrangement there were about a hundred wafers distributed, although the young girls only drew once each; because on this point I was inexorable, not wishing either to favour abuses or to make preferences, which might produce discontent. My wife hinted to those who had lucky numbers to share with their comrades, by means of which the division of spoil was almost equal, and joy was general.

NINTH PROMENADE

I begged the nun to draw in her turn, fearing strongly that she would disdainfully reject my offer; she accepted with a good grace, drew like her pensionnaires, and took forthright what came to her. I was infinitely thankful to her for it, and in this I found a sort of politeness which strongly pleased me, and which was well worth, I believe, that of grimacing affectations. During all this performance, there were disputes which were brought before my tribunal; and these small girls, coming to plead their cause one after the other, gave me occasion to remark, that although there was not one pretty among them, the charm of some made their ugliness forgotten.

We all parted finally well content with each other, and that afternoon was one of those of my life which memory recalls to me with most satisfaction. The feast, for the rest, was not ruinous; for thirty pence that it cost me at the most, I obtained more than a hundred crowns of contentment; so true is it that pleasure is not measured by expense, and that joy is more the friend of pennies than of pounds. I have returned many a time to the same place, at the same time, hoping to find the little troop again; but that has not happened to me.

This recalls to me another amusement of almost the same sort, the remembrance of which comes to me from much farther off. It was in the unhappy time, when misled by the rich and by men of letters I was sometimes reduced to share their dismal pleasures.

I was at La Chevrette at the time of the birthday feast
of the master of the house: all his family were united
to celebrate it, and all the glitter of noisy pleasure was
employed to produce this effect. Theatrical spectacles,
feasts, fireworks, nothing was spared. There was not
the time to draw breath, and one was stunned rather
than amused. After dinner we went to take the
air in the avenue, where a sort of fair was held. A
dance started; the gentlemen condescended to dance
with the peasant girls, but the ladies kept their dignity.
Gingerbread was sold there. A young man of the
company decided to buy some in order to throw them
one after the other in the midst of the crowd; and everyone took so much pleasure in seeing all these clod-
hoppers precipitate themselves, beat each other, throw
each other down in order to have the gingerbread,
that each wished to give himself the same pleasure.
And gingerbreads began flying from right to left,
and girls and boys to run, to fall over each other and to
lame each other. This appeared charming to everybody. I did as the others, out of base shame, but
inwardly I was not amused so much as they. But,
soon weary of emptying my purse to make people
crush each other, I left the good company and went
to walk alone in the fair. The variety of the objects
there amused me for a long time. I perceived among
others five or six boys from Savoy, around a small girl
who had still on her tray a dozen meagre apples, which
she was anxious to get rid of; the Savoyards, on their

side, would have gladly freed her of them; but they had
only two or three pence among them all, and that was
not much to make a great breach amid the apples.
This tray was for them the garden of the Hesperides;
and the young girl was the dragon who guarded it.
This comedy amused me for a long time; I finally
created a climax by paying for the apples from the
young girl and distributing them among the small
boys. I had then one of the finest spectacles that can
flatter a man's heart, that of seeing joy united with the
innocence of youth, spreading everywhere about me.
For the spectators themselves, in seeing it, partook
of it, and I, who shared at such cheap expense this
happiness, had in addition the joy of feeling that it was
my work.

In comparing this amusement with that which I
had just quitted, I felt with satisfaction the difference
which there is between healthy tastes and natural
feelings and those which opulence creates, and which
are scarcely more than pleasures of mockery and ex-
clusive tastes engendered by scorn. For, what sort
of pleasure could one take in seeing troops of men
made vile by misery, fall over each other, stifle themselves, brutally cripple themselves in order to snatch
hastily some morsels of gingerbread trampled by feet
and covered with mud ?

On my part, when I have well reflected on the sort
of pleasure which I tasted on these sorts of occasions,
I have found that it consisted less in a feeling of well-

doing than in the pleasure of seeing happy faces. This sight for me has a charm which, though it penetrates to my heart, seems to be uniquely that of sensation. If I do not see the satisfaction I cause, even when I am sure of it, I only half rejoice. It is even for me a disinterested pleasure, which does not depend on the part which I may have in it; for, in the feasts of the people, that of seeing gay faces has always vividly attracted me. This attempt has, however, often been frustrated in France, where this nation, which pretends to be so gay, shows very little of this gaiety in its looks. Often I went to popular fairs, in order to see the common people dancing; but their dances were so discontented, their mien so sorrowful, so awkward, that I emerged more saddened than rejoiced. But at Geneva and in Switzerland, where laughter does not evaporate incessantly into stupid malignities, all breathes contentment and gaiety at feasts. Misery does not wear its hideous aspect; extravagance does not show its insolence; well-being, brotherhood, concord dispose hearts to expand; and often in the transports of an innocent joy unknown people accost each other, embrace each other and invite each other to enjoy the pleasures of the day together. To enjoy these amiable festivals myself, I have no need to take part in them. It suffices me to see them; in seeing, I partake of them, and among so many gay faces I am sure that there is no heart more gay than mine.

NINTH PROMENADE

Although this is only a pleasure of sensations, it certainly has a moral cause; and the proof is, that this same aspect, instead of flattering me, of pleasing me, can tear me to pieces with sorrow and indignation, when I know that these signs of pleasure and of joy on the faces of evilly-disposed people are nothing but the signs that their malignity is satisfied. Innocent joy is the only one whose signs flatter my heart. Those of cruel and mocking joy break it and afflict it, even though it has nothing to do with me. These signs without a doubt cannot be exactly the same, since they arise from principles so different; but after all, they are equally signs of joy, and their sensible differences are not assuredly proportionate to those of the movements which they excite in me.

Those of sorrow and of grief are still more painful to me, to the point that it is impossible to endure them without being agitated myself with emotions perhaps more acute than those they represent. Imagination, reinforcing sensation, identifies me with the suffering being and often gives me more agony than he feels himself. A discontented face is also a spectacle which it is impossible for me to endure, above all if I have reason to think that this discontent refers to me. I could not say how much the sullen and discontented air of servants who wait upon me reluctantly has snatched from me crowns in the houses where I formerly was stupid enough to let myself be drawn, and where the servants always made me pay dearly for the hospitality of the masters. Always too much moved by sensible objects, and above all by those which bore signs of pleasure or of blame, of benevolence or of aversion, I allowed myself to be led on by these external impressions, without being able ever to escape otherwise than by flight. A sign, a gesture, a glance of the eye, of an unknown man, sufficed to trouble my pleasures or calm my pains. I am not in full possession of myself except when I am alone; outside of this, I am the plaything of all those who surround me.

I lived once with pleasure in the world, when in all eyes I saw nothing but benevolence, or, at the worst, indifference in those to whom I was unknown; but, to-day when they take no less trouble to show my face to the people than to mask my natural character, I cannot put a foot into the road without seeing myself surrounded by disturbing objects. I hasten to gain, with long strides, the country; as soon as I see a little green, I begin to breathe. Should you be astonished that I love solitude? I see nothing but animosity in the visages of men, and nature ever smiles at me.

I feel however, still, it must be admitted, some pleasure in living in the midst of men so long as my face is unknown to them. But this is a pleasure that men leave me rarely. Some years ago I still liked to traverse the villages and to see, in the morning, labourers mending their flails, or women at their gates with their children. This sight had something in it that

touched my heart. I stopped sometimes, without
meaning it, to look at the little households of these
good people, and I found myself sighing without
knowing wherefore. I did not know if anyone saw
me delighting in this small pleasure or if they wish
to deprive me of it; but at the change which I
perceive upon their physiognomies as I pass, and
at the air with which I am regarded, I am forced to
notice that they have taken great care to remove this
incognito for me. The same thing has happened
to me in a more marked fashion at the Invalides.
This fine establishment has always interested me. I
never see without tenderness and veneration these
groups of good old men who can say, like those of
Sparta,

> We have once been
> Young, valiant and hardy.

One of my favorite promenades was about the
Military School, and I encountered with pleasure here
and there certain pensioners who, having retained the
ancient military politeness, saluted me in passing. This
salutation, which my heart gave back to them a hundred-
fold, flattered me and increased the pleasure I had in
seeing them. As I did not know how to conceal anything that touched me, I often spoke of the pensioners
and of the way in which the sight of them moved
me. It was a mistake. At the end of some time,
I perceived that I was not unknown to them, or rather
that I was unfavourably so, because they looked on me

with the same eyes as the public did. No more politeness, no more salutations. A disdainful air, a fierce
look succeeded to their first politeness. The ancient
frankness of their trade not allowing them, like
others, to cover their animosity with a sneering and
traitorous mask, they openly showed me the most
violent hatred; and such is the excess of my misery
that I am forced to distinguish in my esteem those who
disguise the least their fury.

Since then, I walk with less pleasure in the direction
of the Invalides; however, as my sentiments for them
do not depend on theirs for me, I never see without
respect and interest these ancient defenders of their
country; but it is very hard to see myself so badly
repaid on their part for the justice which I render
to them. When, by chance, I encounter someone
who has escaped the common order, or who, not
knowing my face, does not show me any aversion,
his honest salutation recompenses me for the rude
appearance of others. I forget them in order to
occupy myself only with him, and I imagine that
there is one of those souls like mine, into which hatred
cannot penetrate. I still had that pleasure, last year,
when I crossed the water to walk on the Island of
Swans. A poor old pensioner, in a boat, was waiting
for a companion to cross. I presented myself, and
ordered the boatman to start. The water was swift and
the crossing long. I scarcely dared ask the pensioner
a question, for fear of being insulted and rebuffed as

usual: but his polite air reassured me. We talked
together. He appeared to me a man of sense and
of morals. I was surprised and charmed with his
open and affable tone. I was not accustomed to so
much favour. My surprise ceased when I learnt that
he had newly arrived from the province. I understood
that they had not yet pointed out my face to him and
given him his instructions. I profited by this incognito
to talk some moments with a man, and from my
enjoyment I perceived how much the rarity of the
most common pleasures is able to augment their value.
On leaving the boat, he got ready his two poor pennies.
I paid his passage, and begged him to keep his money,
while trembling with fear of annoying him. This did
not happen; on the contrary, he appeared sensible of
my attention, and above all of the fact that, as he was
an older man, I had assisted him to leave the boat.
Who would believe that I was so much a child as to
weep freely ? I was consumed with the wish to put a
coin of twenty-four sous in his hand to buy tobacco;
I did not dare do it. The same shame which held me
back then has often prevented me from doing good
actions, which would have filled me with joy, and from
which I have abstained while deploring my imbecility.
This time, after having quitted my old pensioner, I
soon consoled myself by thinking that I should have
acted against my own principles by mixing with
true things a piece of silver which degrades their
nobility and soils their disinterestedness. We should

haſten to aid those who need it; but, in the ordinary commerce of life, let natural benevolence and urbanity carry out their work, without anything venial or mercantile daring to approach such a pure source to corrupt or spoil it. They say that in Holland people demand payment for telling you the hour and for showing you the road; they muſt be a very despicable people who thus sell the simpleſt rights of humanity.

I have noticed that it is only in Europe that hospitality is sold. In the whole of Asia you are lodged free of charge. I underſtand that there are not so many luxuries; but is it nothing to say: I am a man and have been received among men; is it pure humanity which gives me shelter? Small privations are endured without trouble, when the heart is better treated than the body.

TENTH PROMENADE

TO-DAY, Palm Sunday, it is precisely fifty years since my firſt acquaintance with Madame de Warens. She was twenty-eight then, being born with the century. I was not seventeen, and my awakening temperament, which I ſtill did not underſtand, gave a new warmth to a heart naturally full of life. Since it was not aſtonishing that she should conceive benevolence for a lively young man, who was gentle and modeſt, with an agreeable face, it was less aſtonishing that a charming woman, full of spirit and grace, should inspire me with gratitude, and with more tender sentiments which I did not then diſtinguish.

But, what is less usual is that this firſt moment decided me for all my life, and produced, by an inevitable interlinking, my deſtiny for the reſt of my days. My soul, the moſt precious faculties of which my organs had not developed, had no determined form. It waited in a sort of impatience for the moment which should give it one, and this moment, accelerated by this encounter, did not come so soon; and in the simplicity of morals which education had given me, I saw prolonged in me for a long time this delicious but rapid state in which love and innocence inhabit the same heart. She had sent me away. Everything recalled me to her; I had to return.

This return determined my fate, and long before possessing her, I only lived in her and for her. Ah! if I had sufficed her heart as she sufficed mine, what peaceful and delicious days we should have passed together! We did pass such days; but they were short and swift, and what a destiny has followed them! There is not a day when I do not remember with joy and tenderness this unique and brief time of my life, when I was fully myself, without mixture and without obstacle, and when I can truly say I lived.

I might say, a little like that pretorian prefect, who, disgraced under Vespasian, went to finish peaceably his days in the country: " I have spent seventy years upon earth, and I have lived seven." But for this short but precious space I should have remained perhaps uncertain of myself; because all the rest of my life, easily and without resistance, I have been so agitated, shaken, almost passive, that in so stormy a life I should have difficulty in distinguishing what is mine in my own conduct, so much has hard necessity continued to weigh upon me. But during this short number of years, loved by a woman full of complaisance and sweetness, I did what I wished to do, I was that which I wished to be, and by the use which I made of my leisure, aided by her lessons and her example, I was able to give my soul, still simple and new, the form which belonged to it despite everything, and which it has kept for ever.

The taste for solitude and contemplation was born in my heart with the expansive and tender sentiments made to be its food. Tumult and noise restricted and stifled them; calm and peace reanimated and exalted them.

I need to concentrate myself in order to love. I persuaded Mamma to live in the country. An isolated house on the slope of a valley was our refuge; and it was there that, for the space of four or five years, I enjoyed a century of life and of pure and full happiness, which covers with its charm all that my lot presents of frightful fact. I needed a mistress according to my heart; I possessed her. I wanted the country; I obtained it. I could not endure subjection; I was perfectly free, and more than free, because, subjected by my attachment alone, I only did what I wished to do. All my time was filled with affectionate cares or with country occupations. I did not desire anything but the continuation of a state so sweet; my one grief was the fear that it would not last for long, and this fear, born of the worry of our situation, was not without foundation.

From thenceforward I tried to picture myself both diversions from this disquiet, and resources to atone for its ill results. I thought that a store of talents was the surest resource against indigence, and I resolved to employ my leisure in putting myself, if it were possible, in a position to return one day to the best of women the assistance which I had received from her. . . .

[No more was written; Rousseau died a few weeks later.]